Guns of Wrath

Will Comfort has a burning mission: to wreak vengeance on the man who had him incarcerated during the Civil War. The quest brings him to the river town of Cayuse Landing where he soon runs foul of the ruthless rancher, Rank Wilder. Comfort is increasingly drawn into the conflict between Wilder and the local townsfolk until he has to face the question: who is his real enemy?

Others are caught up, including Annie, the woman from his past, Corrina, the woman in his present, the oldster 'Beaver' Bannock and the Reverend Bent. Comfort is not the only one to have to confront what he believes in and where his loyalties lie, as violence continues to escalate.

Guns of Wrath

Colin Bainbridge

A Black Horse Western

ROBERT HALE · LONDON

© Colin Bainbridge 2011
First published in Great Britain 2011

ISBN 978-0-7090-9300-8

Robert Hale Limited
Clerkenwell House
Clerkenwell Green
London EC1R 0HT

www.halebooks.com

Typeset by
Derek Doyle & Associates, Shaw Heath
Printed and bound in Great Britain by
CPI Antony Rowe, Chippenham and Eastbourne

CHAPTER ONE

Sounds of laughter and broken snatches of conversation floated up from the garden as Miss Annie's girls enjoyed their Sunday break. They had returned from church not long before; not the main church, which most of the respectable citizens attended, but the tent on the outskirts of town where the self-styled Reverend Abraham Bent held his weekly meetings. It was part of her care to ensure that they attended regularly. Today, they looked and behaved just like any other young women, Miss Annie reflected; dressed in their linen and gingham dresses, they were almost unrecognizable as the girls of the Crystal Arcade saloon. She smiled as she lit a cigar, turned away from the window above the garden at the back of the building, crossed the room and took a seat on the wooden balcony overlooking the street at the front. The house was on the edge of the settlement where the trail leading down from the high country abruptly became the main street of dusty false-framed structures that formed the town of Cayuse Landing. At the opposite side of town flowed the Old

Muddy river. Miss Annie's first establishment had been a floating hog ranch. The Crystal Arcade was arguably an improvement, but only just.

As she observed the quiet Sunday scene, a rider came into view down the trail. He was still quite a long way off and his horse, a sorrel gelding, was stepping slowly so that it took some time before she was able to see him more clearly. He wore a grey shirt with a waistcoat and dusty black chaps. He was not wearing a hat; his rumpled dark hair was streaked with grey and his sallow cheeks and chin wore a dark shadow. As he approached he caught sight of her and looked up. She gave an involuntary start. Surely there couldn't be anyone else with those steely blue eyes? Had he recognized her? The only sign he gave was to touch the corner of his brow with his finger. It was a conventional greeting and the next moment he had passed her and was carrying on riding slowly and deliberately up the main street. She watched him till he passed the Crystal Arcade, and then she realized that the cigar was fixed in her mouth. She took it out and blew a cloud of smoke into the air. Could she have been mistaken? She didn't think so. Unless she was way wrong, that rider was Will Comfort. It had been a long time. A lot of water had flowed under the bridge. She hadn't heard anything of him for years. So what could have brought him to Cayuse Landing?

Will Comfort drew his horse to a halt outside the Crystal Arcade, dismounted and tied it to the hitch rail. With a glance up and down the street, he stepped through the batwing doors. The place was quiet. A few people sat at tables playing cards and there was a group of three standing at the bar. The bartender looked up at his approach and it seemed to Comfort that he looked more than a little apprehensive.

'Howdy,' he said. 'What'll it be?'

'Whiskey.'

The bartender poured a glass. He placed it on the counter and Comfort slung it back.

'Another,' he said.

The bartender obliged. While he was doing so Comfort took the opportunity to take a close look at the place through the mirror behind the bar.

'Kinda quiet,' he said.

'Yeah. It's Sunday. The girls have a day off. It'll get busier later.' Comfort took another drink, but slowly this time. The man next to him glanced up.

'Stranger in town?' he asked.

Comfort turned as he put his foot on the bar-rail. The man was small and strangely wizened. Until he spoke, Comfort had barely noticed him.

'Yup.'

'Fixin' to stay or just passin' through?'

'That depends.'

The man was about to reply when a deep voice from behind Comfort broke into the conversation.

'Depends on what?'

Comfort looked in the mirror. The voice belonged to a tall, wiry individual with a scar running down his left cheek. He was wearing a buscadero gunbelt tied low with a thong and he carried two guns. Just behind him the third man at the bar began to move away. He was shorter and more stocky but he carried the same armaments.

'I'd say that was my business,' Comfort said.

'I'd say not,' the man replied.

The bartender looked more anxious than ever. 'Why don't you two gentlemen have a drink on the house?' he suggested.

Nobody responded. Comfort raised his glass of whiskey to his lips and turned back to the little man who was just behind him.

'Care for a drink?' he said.

'Why, sure.'

Ignoring the two men on his other side, Comfort turned to the barman.

'Just give me the bottle,' he said.

The barman glanced nervously at the two gunnies and then reached for the bottle and placed it on the counter. The deep voice rasped out again.

'You can pour a drink for me and Jud before you walk back out the door.'

Comfort poured two drinks for himself and the oldster.

'Sure appreciate it,' the oldster said.

Comfort was keeping an eye on things in the mirror. Looking at the oldster's reflection, he could see no sign of fear. Suddenly the gunnie lunged at Comfort and spun him round by the shoulder.

'Start walkin' now or you're a dead man,' he said.

Comfort stared at him for a moment and then turned back to the bar.

'I said, start walkin',' the man snapped.

8

Comfort raised his glass and took a long swallow; the oldster did likewise. As he put the glass on the counter the gunnie's hand swept to his holster but Comfort was too quick for him. Before the gun was in the man's hand, Comfort's Dragoon was spitting lead and the man was lifted back to crash against the bar. Almost in the same motion Comfort swung round; his third and fourth shots took the other man in the chest as his own gun exploded, sending a bullet thudding harmlessly into the ceiling. The next moment there was another stab of flame and the roar of gunfire. Comfort dropped instinctively to one knee; the oldster had a smoking gun in his hand and was looking towards a corner of the room. Comfort followed the line of his gaze to see another man clutching at his stomach and looking with a shocked expression at the oldster. For a few moments he continued to stand, then he fell face forward, clattering into the table at which he had been sitting and bringing it crashing to the floor with him. Comfort glanced at the oldster.

'He went for his gun along with those two,' the oldster said.

'Thanks. I guess I owe you.'

He straightened up and stepped over to where the other two were lying. One glance told him they were both dead. He became aware of movement in the room. Some of the customers were coming forward and the barman seemed to have recovered his wits.

'You saw what happened,' Comfort said. 'Somebody better go and get the marshal.' He was placing his gun back into his gunbelt when the oldster grabbed him by the arm.

9

'Never mind waitin' for the marshal,' he snapped. 'Better get out of here.'

He tugged at Comfort's arm and Comfort allowed himself to be led away. As they approached the batwings the oldster suddenly walked back and took the bottle of whiskey.

'You paid for it,' he said. 'Seems a pity to let it go to waste.'

They came out into the sunlight. A few people had gathered on the opposite side of the street.

'Where's your hoss?' the oldster said.

'Right here,' Comfort replied.

'Mine too. Let's get goin'.'

Matching action to his words, the oldster leaped on to the back of a skewbald Pinto. Comfort did likewise and they set off at a gallop, kicking up dust as they careered down the street. The oldster took a turning and Comfort followed suit, aware as he did so that somebody was shouting after him. He took a quick glance backward. A man who might have been the marshal had appeared on the scene and was waving a gun in the air. The next moment they had rounded another corner and were out in the open country, heading for the hills.

They continued to ride hard until they had put distance between them and the town, when at last they slowed up. The oldster came alongside Comfort; there was a big lopsided grin on his face which revealed for the first time a pair of prominent front teeth that rested on his lower lip.

'Tarnation!' he said. 'I never expected nothin' like that.'

'Thanks again for backin' me up,' Comfort said. 'I never took no account of that other one. If you hadn't taken care of him they'd probably be cartin' me off to boot hill as well as them.'

'My pleasure,' the oldster replied. 'And I mean that. Those Drewitt boys been gettin' away with it for too long. It's about time somebody stood up to them.' Comfort raised himself in his stirrups to examine their back trail.

'No sign of anybody,' he said.

'The marshal ain't likely to get up a posse,' the oldster replied.

'You seemed to be mighty keen to get away from the place,' Comfort said.

'Yeah.' He looked up at the sky. 'Look,' he continued, 'it's gettin' dark. We'll ride on further and make camp in a place I know where nobody won't find us. Then I can explain.'

'Ain't got any better idea,' Comfort said.

'Before we go any further, maybe we'd better make some introductions. Name's Beaver, Beaver Bannock. Leastways, that's what they've always called me, for obvious reasons. Guess Beaver weren't the name my mother gave me, but I'm plumb danged if I can remember any other.' He grinned again, exposing again his two prominent front teeth.

'And my name's Comfort, Will Comfort. Pleased to make your acquaintance.'

They shook hands and the oldster laughed.

'Guess you didn't make things too comfortable for those varmints in the Crystal Arcade,' he said.

'It was their doin', not mine,' Comfort retorted.

The oldster's burst of merriment subsided. 'Come on,' he said. 'We got more ridin' to put in.'

It was dark and they were well into the hills before Beaver rode down into a hollow overhung with willow and cottonwood trees, where a narrow stream murmured in the undergrowth. They soon had a fire going and bacon and beans simmering in a pan. Comfort filled the blackened kettle with water from the stream. When they had eaten and were on their second cup of steaming thick coffee, Comfort produced his pouch of Bull Durham and they rolled cigarettes. The night was warm and a soft breeze rustled the leaves.

'OK,' Comfort said, lying back and resting his head against his saddle. 'Perhaps you'd better tell me just what that was all about.'

'I take it you're referring to that little altercation in the Crystal Arcade?'

'What else?' Comfort replied.

The oldster took a long drag on his cigarette and sighed with satisfaction as he blew the smoke out.

'That sure feels good,' he said. 'I ain't had a decent smoke in months.'

'You hit hard times?' Comfort asked.

'You could say that, except I been hittin' 'em for years now.'

'You live in Cayuse Landing?'

'Much as you could say I live anywhere. I got a little shack on the other side of town. I do a bit of work at the saloon, swampin' out, runnin' messages for the girls, that sort of thing. It ain't much of a livin'.'

12

'You were pretty good with that gun.'

The oldster looked animated.

'Yeah, it wasn't always this way. I got you to thank for gettin' me to do somethin' for a change.'

'Like I say, you're pretty good with a gun.'

'I practise. Helps put in the time when I'm out at the shack and I ain't seen nobody for awhiles.'

'So who were those varmints? Seems like it didn't take much to upset 'em. They were just lookin' for a fight.'

'Those three don't count for nothin'. There's plenty others just like them. They ride for an outfit called the Black Stirrup. It's run by an *hombre* name of Rank Wilder. Him and his gang just about run the town. The marshal is nothin' but a stooge. That's why I had to get you away from there. You'd have been thrown straight in the slammer if they hadn't of lynched you.'

'Doesn't anybody do somethin' about it?'

'Folks is too scared. Hell, I've been runnin' scared myself until today.'

'From what you've said about the marshal and all, you ain't gonna be able to go back.'

The oldster looked slyly at Comfort.

'Guess not. Less'n maybe you'd consider ridin' back too.'

Comfort laughed.

'Me! Nope, whatever's goin' on in Cayuse Landing, it ain't none of my business.'

The oldster drew another cloud of smoke into his lungs.

'So what is your business?' he said. 'What was it

13

brought you to Cayuse Landing? I seem to remember you sayin' about it dependin' on something.'

'Yeah, but it ain't nothin' for you to concern yourself about.'

'Reckon I'd like to know just the same. Maybe I could help.'

Comfort leaned forward and poured himself another cup of coffee. He sat up, placing his back against the saddle.

'Now you come to mention it,' he said, 'maybe you could.'

'Go ahead, I'm listenin'.'

Comfort spent a moment gathering his thoughts.

'You fought in the war?' he said at length.

The oldster nodded.

'Sure did. Seen plenty of action. Got invalided out after Murfreesboro.'

'You were the lucky one,' Comfort said. 'I spent two years in a prisoner of war camp. Name of Jasperstown.'

The oldster looked closely at Comfort.

'Hell,' he said. 'Don't know about that place, but I heard Andersonville was real bad.'

'Hell's the right word,' Comfort responded. 'It was hell on earth. I don't want to talk about it. The commandant was a man called Laidler. I knew a lot of good men that never came out of that place alive. Some did but they might as well have been dead. To cut a long story short, there were two people come out swearing revenge on Laidler. Their names were Briggs and Comfort.'

'The war was a long time ago,' Bannock said.

14

'That don't mean Laidler ain't got it comin' to him. Just means it's been kinda delayed.'

The oldster glanced again at his companion. His lips were curled almost in a snarl and even in the flickering light of the fire he could see a nerve twitch in his cheek.

'What took you so long to catch up with him?'

'Ain't caught up with him yet, but it won't take much more time.'

'So why the delay?'

Comfort shrugged. 'You know how it is,' he said. 'Things get in the way.'

The oldster nodded. 'Yeah, I know what you mean,' he replied. 'Look at me. I wasn't always swampin' out in some two-bit saloon.'

Comfort shifted his position once more.

'Wasted years,' Bannock mused, more to himself than to Comfort. 'Best not to think about 'em.' He looked across at his companion again. 'Still don't explain what you were doin' in Cayuse Landin'.'

Comfort seemed to make an almost physical effort to draw himself together.

'Like I was sayin',' he continued, 'the two of us swore an oath we'd get even with Laidler. We went our separate ways once we got out of that camp, but we swore we'd meet up after six months and set about trackin' Laidler down once we'd kinda got our affairs back in order.'

'Track him down? What happened to him? Ain't he doin' time for what he did?'

'He was too clever for that. He got away just before the Federals liberated us.'

'What happened when you met up?'

'We didn't. That was my fault. I was the one missed the rendezvous. There was nothin' I could do about it.'

'Let me guess. You were servin' time yourself?'

Comfort summoned a wan smile.

'Not on that occasion,' he said. 'No, I was laid up with a bad bout of fever. Guess I was lucky to pull through. Couldn't have done it without a lot of help. By the time I got back on my feet the chance was gone. After that, like I say, things got kinda complicated and I lost touch with Briggs. Just recently I got information concernin' him. I had reasons for thinkin' he might have been in Cayuse Landin' quite recently.'

He turned to the oldster. 'Does the name mean anythin' to you?' Bannock's brows puckered. 'Nope,' he said after a few moments thought, 'can't say the name rings any bells.'

'Don't necessarily mean anythin',' Comfort replied. 'He could be usin' a different name.'

'Why would he do that?' Bannock said.

'I don't know. Just a supposition,' Comfort replied. 'I'm considerin' any possibility.'

Silence descended as each man dwelt on his own thoughts. The fire had died down and the circle of darkness outside the firelight seemed to grow blacker. The ripple of the stream sounded further away and from a long distance there came the lonesome cry of a nightjar.

'Well,' Comfort said, 'I don't know about you but I'm gettin' a mite tired. Reckon I'll turn in for the night.'

'Sure, you do that,' the oldster replied. 'I'll just sit

16

here and kinda keep watch for a while.'

'You figure that's necessary?'

'Probably not.'

'Make sure you wake me up later and get some sleep yourself,' Comfort replied.

He moved his gear a little distance from the fire and lay down. In a matter of minutes he was asleep.

Bannock pulled his knees up and watched the fire as it gradually dwindled. He was feeling strange and didn't know what interpretation to put on it. He concluded that in the main it was because for the first time in a long while he had acted decisively. For too long he had been playing the part of town bum, content to let Wilder and his gang of gunslicks treat him with amused contempt. In that instant when he had drawn his six-gun in defence of Will Comfort, he had changed that situation irretrievably. He felt good about it, although he didn't know now to what it might lead. And who was this man Comfort? He had appeared from nowhere and he knew nothing about him. From what Comfort had said, he gathered that he had spent at least part of the previous seven years since the War in jail. That had to be one reason for the lapse of time between him being liberated from the internment camp and getting on the trail of this *hombre* Laidler. What crime had he committed? He didn't feel apprehensive. There was something about Comfort that engendered trust. And it had been something to see the way he had handled Wilder's gunnies in the Crystal Arcade. He found himself suddenly thinking of Miss Annie. It was just as well that her girls had missed the altercation, although he had a sneaking feeling that Miss Annie might have felt differently, might indeed have felt something like he did.

He got to his feet, intending, like Comfort, to turn in for the night, when he stopped in his tracks. He had heard a sound like the snapping of a twig. His first instinct was to warn Comfort, but on second thoughts he slipped into the shelter of the surrounding trees, drawing his six-gun as he did so. He listened intently but it was not repeated and he was beginning to think he must be mistaken when he heard something else, this time the unmistakable sound of a shoe scuffing the ground. The horses began to stamp and one of them snorted. Whoever was approaching the camp wasn't making a very good job of keeping undetected. A minute passed. He glanced across the clearing towards the supine figure of Comfort, half-expecting him to awaken but he showed no sign of stirring. In another moment the bushes to his right rustled and parted and someone crept out into the faint glow of the fading embers. Bannock was about to step out of cover when Comfort suddenly sat up and Bannock caught a gleam of light from the gun he held in his hand.

'OK, stop right there!' Comfort snapped.

Bannock, taking his cue, moved forward into the open.

'Better do exactly as he says,' he said to the intruder.

The shadowy figure stopped dead in its tracks.

'Don't shoot,' a voice said. 'I come as a friend.'

Bannock wondered whether Comfort was as surprised as he was. The voice was that of a woman.

18

'Put your hands in the air!' Comfort ordered.

The woman did as requested. Comfort took a couple of steps towards her, then stopped. Bannock was expecting him to do or say something but for a few moments he just stood as if transfixed to the spot.

'Annie,' he said at last. 'Annie O'Reilly! Is it really you?'

The woman's back was towards Bannock but now he recognized her too as Miss Annie from the Crystal Arcade.

'Yes, it's me. And I knew I couldn't be mistaken. I knowed it was you, Will Comfort, as soon as I saw you come ridin' into town.'

'The woman on the balcony,' Comfort said. 'It was you!'

The next moment Comfort had taken a last step forward and Miss Annie was in his arms. They held each other for just a moment, then, as they moved apart, Bannock, feeling just a little foolish, walked towards them. The group stood together, illuminated in the dwindling glow of the fire, and none of them seemed sure of what to say next. It was Bannock who took the practical approach.

'Miss Annie, what are you doin' here? You were takin' a chance coming into camp like that.'

'I'm sorry,' she replied. 'I wasn't sure what to do once I got near. I left my horse and walked the last part. I wasn't even entirely certain it was you.'

'You two know each other?' Comfort said.

'Sure. Miss Annie is part owner of the Crystal Arcade. She and her girls . . .'

He hesitated and Miss Annie completed the sentence for him.

'Provide the entertainment,' she added.

Bannock looked from Miss Annie to Comfort.

'I take it you are acquainted as well?' he said.

Comfort put his arm round Miss Annie's shoulder and squeezed her again.

'Yup, we sure are. We used to know each other well. Remember how I was tellin' you about the time I had a real bad bout of fever. I said I couldn't have got through it without a lot of help. Well, it was Miss Annie pulled me back from the brink and nursed me back to health again.'

'It was a bad time,' Miss Annie said. 'It wasn't long after the war and you were still sufferin' its effects.'

'That was a bad time for everybody,' Bannock interjected.

'So how did you wind up in a place like Cayuse Landing?' Comfort said to Miss Annie.

'It's a long story,' she said.

'More to the point,' Bannock said, repeating himself. 'What are you doin' here now?'

Miss Annie looked into Comfort's weathered features.

'I saw him ride into town. Shortly after I heard the shooting. I watched as the pair of you ran out of the saloon and took off for the hills. Figured you might need some provisions. So I packed a few things and here I am.'

'Where did you leave your horse?' Bannock said.

'Back aways, tied to some trees just off the trail.'

20

Bannock turned to Comfort. 'You and Miss Annie make yourselves comfortable. I'll go and bring in the horse.' The oldster's face broke into a grin, exposing his prominent teeth as he turned to Miss Annie. 'You sure are some lady,' he said.

By the time they had settled down for the night, dawn was not far away. When it came they made a good breakfast from the supplies Miss Annie had brought. While they were drinking coffee Miss Annie looked at them in turn.

'Well,' she said, 'it's sure been good to catch up on things, but just what are you boys intending to do next?'

'To some extent, that depends on you,' Comfort replied.

For a moment Bannock thought he detected a glimmer in Miss Annie's eyes.

'How do you mean?' she said.

'Well, I told you and Bannock somethin' about the reason I happen to be in Cayuse Landing. I'm lookin' for a fella name of Briggs, Lonnie Briggs. Are you quite sure you haven't heard the name? I got word he was in the area.'

'Nope, don't mean nothin' to me,' Bannock reiterated.

Miss Annie looked thoughtful.

'I don't know the name,' she said, 'but I been thinkin'. What does this fella look like?'

'It's a long time since I seen him. By the time we were set free he was in a bad way. He was pretty average, I'd say.'

'Was there anythin' distinctive about him?'

21

Comfort suddenly grinned.

'Yeah, come to think of it, there was somethin'. He'd taken a hit at Gaines' Mill. He had a scar. It was in kind of a funny place. He didn't like anyone to mention it in case it looked like he'd had his back to the enemy.'

Miss Annie nodded. 'No need to be coy,' she said. 'That scar was on his backside, wasn't it?'

A crease had appeared in Comfort's brow.

'Yeah, it was,' he said. 'But how would you know about it?'

Miss Annie smiled briefly. 'Let's say one of the girls mentioned it to me,' she said.

'So Briggs has been in Cayuse Landing. When was this?'

'Just hold steady. It might not be the same man. This is all kinda flimsy.'

'Can't be too many *hombres* with a scarred up butt,' Bannock mumbled.

'It was about a week ago. I'm tryin' to remember.'

'Did this girl say anythin' else?' Comfort said.

'No. Only that he treated her nicely and wasn't shy of splashin' some money. She was a little disappointed he didn't come back. Guess he must have been passin' through.'

'Where did you get the information that he was in Cayuse Landing?' Bannock said. 'Seems a mite strange if he was only passin' through.'

'Someone I met in St Louis. He'd known Briggs before the War. Said the last he'd heard of him he was workin' on the river near Cayuse Landing.'

'Could be on the steamboats,' Bannock said.

Comfort thought hard. 'What's the next town down river?' he asked.

'Willow,' Miss Annie replied. 'And Tidesville the other way.'

'OK,' Comfort said. 'I figure this is what I'll do. Ride down to Willow and get me a ticket from there to . . . what was it?'

'Tidesville.'

'OK, Tidesville. That should give me time to find out if Briggs is workin' the boats. If he's not, I might be able to pick up some information.'

'You'd be comin' back through Cayuse Crossin',' the oldster said. 'Better be careful. Rank Wilder ain't gonna be too happy about what happened to the Drewitt boys at the Crystal Arcade.'

Miss Annie turned to Comfort.

'You'd better be careful anyway,' she said. 'Wilder controls most of the river traffic as well as the town and the Black Stirrup.'

'This Wilder seems to figure a lot around here,' Comfort said, 'but my quarrel ain't with him.'

'Not unless he decides to make himself your problem,' Bannock replied.

Comfort got to his feet. 'What about you, Annie?' he said.

'I guess I'd better get on back to the Crystal Arcade,' she replied. 'I got my girls to take care of.' She hesitated for a moment. 'You know where I'm to be found,' she added.

Comfort nodded and turned to Bannock.

'You fancy a river ride?' he said.

'I was hopin' you'd say that,' the oldster replied. 'Sure do. Guess I ain't got much choice anyways now that Wilder's got my number.'

'Sorry you had to get involved,' Comfort said. 'Guess it kinda makes things hot for you in Cayuse Landin'.'

'No apologies needed,' the oldster said. 'I been owin' Wilder a long time. Just wished I'd stood up to him before.'

They saddled up. Miss Annie was the first to ride out. She turned and waved, then disappeared from view round a bend.

'Yup,' Bannock drawled, 'she's quite a woman.'

Comfort climbed into leather.

'Come on,' he said. 'Time we hit the trail to Willow.'

The oldster poured the last of the coffee on the ashes of the fire. He scuffed them with his boot heel.

'OK,' he replied. 'Let's ride.'

CHAPTER TWO

The landing stage at Willow presented a bustling scene of movement and activity. Wagons and buggies were passing up and down and groups of people stood on the quay, either waiting to go aboard the approaching boat or seeing off other passengers. Crates and boxes of various shapes and sizes were lined up, waiting to be carried on deck, together with hogsheads, casks and cases. The river flowed brown and muddy, carrying upon it an occasional tree branch or log; looking down on it, Comfort took a last draw on his cigarette, then flicked the stub into the water. He looked upstream where the shoreline took a bend and saw a whiff of steam above the treetops. A whistle blew and then the prow of the boat appeared. The stern wheel turned, churning up the water and a swelling wave slapped against the side of the quay. There was a crush of people pressing forward to get a look at the approaching craft and Comfort found himself pushed against a young woman wearing a dark cape and a bonnet. She must have been standing behind him but he had not noticed her before.

'Sorry, ma'am', he said, raising his hat.

She smiled and he couldn't help but notice the dimples which appeared in her cheeks.

'It wasn't your fault,' she replied.

Their eyes held their glance a moment longer till the voice of Bannock interrupted them.

'Sure seems to be a lot of folk travellin' today,' he said.

Comfort turned to him.

'Yeah. More than I would have expected.'

The woman looked up at him again.

'I think a lot of folks are heading for the county fair at Tidesville,' she said. 'That's where we're going.'

'We?' Comfort involuntarily replied.

'Yes, me and my brother. He's collecting our luggage.'

Just at that moment a young man appeared. He was slim and his blond hair was tousled. He seemed to be slightly agitated as he struggled with two big bags.

'That's a lot of luggage to be takin' for a day out at the fair,' Comfort said.

'Oh, we're not just going to the fair. Our uncle lives in Tidesville and we're going to spend a few days with him.'

The boat was drawing towards the landing stage.

'Well, I hope you'll have a good time,' Comfort said, and turning to the boy: 'Here; let me give you a hand with those things.'

The boat had docked. The gangway swung out and Comfort took one of the cases. They passed on to the boat and after some moments of confusion, found a seat in the lounge.

'Thanks for your help,' the woman said.

'It weren't nothin',' Comfort replied.

He turned to go. The woman smiled again.

'My name's Corrina,' she said. 'Corrina Stead, and my brother's name is Daniel.'

'Comfort, Will Comfort. And this here is Mr Beaver Bannock.'

Corrina looked at the oldster with a slightly puzzled expression on her face. Bannock grinned.

'Real nice to make your acquaintance,' he said.

Comfort turned and made his way to the door. Outside, he leaned against the rail and watched the flurry of activity which was taking place on the quayside. People were waving as the last straggling passengers came on board. Among them was a man with a drooping black moustache and a stubbled chin. He looked up as he approached and Comfort had a vague feeling that he had seen him before. The man's glance passed over him like a cold ray of steel and then he vanished among the people crowding the decks. The whistle blew and amid a churning of paddle wheels and a billowing of smoke, the steamer put out into the river.

Corrina Stead leaned over the side of the paddle steamer and gazed at the passing scene. All about her the boat was crowded with a motley array of passengers and freight. The decks were filled with wagons, horses, mules, boxes, barrels and tents and all manner of equipment. There was some jostling behind her and suddenly she became aware that she was no longer alone. A man had come up beside her. She glanced at him. He was unshaven and his hair was lank. He smelt of whiskey.

'Now what's a young lady like you doin' all by yourself? Reckon you could do with some company.'

She became aware of his arm around her waist.

'Leave me alone,' she said.

'Now that's no way to behave,' he slurred. 'In fact, I'd call that downright unmannerly.'

'Call it what you want,' she said, 'but take your arm away from me this instant.'

The man laughed and his hand moved up alongside her breast.

'I know you don't mean that,' he said.

Corrina made to move away but he held her tight.

'Now don't go and spoil things,' he said. 'You and I could have a real good time. I can show you all the sights when we hit landfall.'

Corrina was trying to decide what to do. She could humour him, but it was not in her nature. On the other hand she didn't want to let the matter go any further. The stranger looked mean. She had no desire to get her brother involved. She made to move away again but he had wedged her tight against the side of the boat.

'I'll ask once more,' she said. 'Go away and leave me alone.'

Again the man commenced a menacing laugh, but this it was broken into by a voice from behind them both.

'You heard what the lady said.'

Corrina looked round to see Comfort. What she was

most aware of was his piercing blue eyes which at that moment were fixed on her molester with an unwavering intensity. The man seemed momentarily nonplussed by this unexpected intervention, but then his mouth bent in an ugly snarl and his hand moved away from her towards a six-gun, which she now noticed for the first time hanging at his side.

'I wouldn't do that,' Comfort said.

For a second the man seemed to consider this advice, but then his hand moved towards the handle of his gun. Quick as he was, Comfort was quicker. Without a pause he raised his arm and brought his hand slicing down on the gunman's wrist. The gun fell from his hand and before he could do anything else a swinging right fist caught him under the chin. His head snapped back, then he slid to the deck. Comfort bent, picked up the gun and threw it over the side of the vessel.

'I'm sorry you've been troubled, ma'am,' he said.

Corrina had recovered her composure.

'I thank you for your assistance,' she said.

'I don't think he'll be troubling you further.' He paused, unsure how to proceed. 'Can I escort you back to your brother?' he suggested.

'No, thank you. It's very kind of you but I think I'd just like to be alone for a few minutes.'

She moved away.

'Are you sure you'll be OK?'

She nodded and smiled. Comfort watched her progress along the deck, then glanced down at the hunched form of the man who had accosted her. Nobody seemed to have taken any notice of the altercation. He bent down and slapped the man across the face. After a few moments his eyes opened and he shook his head. Comfort grabbed him by the collar and hauled him to his feet. He recognized him now as the man he had observed coming up the gangway, and he thought he remembered where he had seen him before. He had a feeling that he had been in the Crystal Arcade on the occasion of the gunfight. He had no way of knowing whether he had been with the Drewitt boys, but in view of his current behaviour it seemed quite likely.

'You remember me?' Comfort said.

The man wiped his hand across his mouth. He was still drunk but through the fumes of alcohol he was trying to piece things together.

'You're lucky I don't throw you overboard,' Comfort said.

The man's lip curled in a snarl of hatred.

'You'll pay for this,' he hissed.

Comfort was thinking. If he was right about the man having been at the Crystal Arcade, had he been with the Drewitt boys? Was his presence on the boat not just a coincidence? He decided to try and surprise the man.

'Tell Wilder to keep out of my way,' he said.

The man had gained something of his senses, but not enough to hide his confusion and the attempt to cover it.

'Wilder,' he stuttered. 'I don't know nobody called Wilder. Who the hell—'

He made to brush past Comfort but Comfort pushed him back against the rail.

'Even more to the point,' he said, 'you'd better make sure I never see you again. Next time I might not be so lenient.'

With a last look into the man's face, he turned away and started to make for the bar. There was no doubt in his mind that the man was one of Wilder's boys. The only thing he wasn't sure about was whether his presence on the boat was coincidental, or whether he was acting on Wilder's orders. From what he knew of people like Wilder, he wouldn't let a matter like the shoot-out in the Crystal Arcade go unpunished. People like Wilder couldn't afford to let anyone get away with anything that might undermine their authority. The more he thought about it, the more he had a feeling that his account with this particular *hombre* was still unsettled.

Night came down. On shore a few scattered lights indicated the presence of a tiny settlement or some isolated ranch house. The moon hung low, obscured by scudding clouds. Comfort had left Bannock finishing his meal. He had been tempted to try his hand at a game of poker but the noise and commotion had sent him back on deck. He found himself thinking of Corrina Stead. He had hoped he might see her again but since the incident with the drunk she had made herself scarce. He guessed she had taken a cabin. It would probably be easy to check on her travelling arrangements, but they were none of his business. By noon the next day they should be back in Cayuse Landing.

From there he and Bannock would travel as far as the

next town. He saw no point in going any further. Bannock had been making some discreet enquiries but had been unsuccessful in picking up any information about a man called Briggs. None of the crew was called by that name. Comfort wasn't too bothered. It was a long shot, after all. It would have been too much to expect that anyone would have heard about Briggs, much less that he might even have been working on the boat. But it was worth a try. Sooner or later something would give and he would find him.

A cool wind blew across Comfort's face. Muffled sounds came from the saloon and patches of light dappled the deck. The paddle wheels throbbed and the long line of the boat's wake cut the surface of the water like a furrow.

Lulled by the steady rhythm of the wheels, Comfort was only vaguely aware of another splashing sound and didn't register that anything had occurred till he saw a glimmer of something red in the water. He looked down, attracted by movement. Something was threshing about. He thought he heard a faint cry, then the realization hit him that someone was in the river.

Without hesitation he climbed over the rail and plunged into the water. He hit the surface with an ungainly splat. Something like a giant hand seemed to grip him and pull him under, forcing him down and down despite his desperate efforts to escape and rise to the surface. He looked up and saw a gigantic shape like a leviathan passing over him and he was sucked down even further. A dark shadow loomed above him. It was the paddle wheel and he was buffeted like a fallen leaf in the vortex.

He kicked his legs and felt himself begin to rise but the surface seemed a long way off. His lungs were bursting and he had given up hope of coming to the top when suddenly his head broke through and he began to gulp the marvellous air into his lungs in desperate mouthfuls.

He turned his head. The giant shape of the boat had pulled away and he became aware of the red object struggling in the water nearby. After a moment the object disappeared. Taking as much air into his lungs as he could hold, Comfort dived again beneath the surface. For a moment he could see nothing in the murky gloom and then he saw the object of his search slowly sinking towards the depths. He kicked out and succeeded in getting an arm round the man's neck. Kicking desperately, Comfort sought to bring him to the surface. The man was limp and heavy but as they emerged he began to thrash and struggle. Comfort shouted as loudly as he could for the man to desist and he must have heard because his struggles died down and instead he lay back, his head just above water and his shoulders supported by Comfort.

Comfort looked about, trying to get his bearings. The night was black but there was a faint flickering gleam to his left and he decided to try and make for it. He lay back, kicking his feet and straining to keep the other man afloat. It was hard going and he was beginning to think they would never make it when unexpectedly his feet touched bottom. Half-swimming and half-walking, he struggled onwards and began to rise out of the water. He realized that he had come on a sandbank and that the light he had seen was a buoy indicating the channel. In a few moments he was out of the water, dragging the other man with him. Only when he laid him on the sand did he give an involuntary gasp. It was Bannock! The oldster began to cough and splutter violently. Comfort laid him on his chest and began to pump and massage his back in a desperate effort to expel the water from his lungs. It seemed to take a long time but then Bannock's head turned and he looked up at his rescuer.

'Are you gonna be OK?' Comfort said.

The oldster managed to nod his head. After a few more moments his teeth glimmered in the darkness and Comfort surmised he was attempting a grin.

'That steamboat,' he whispered. 'I sure don't think much of the service.'

He kneeled for a few moments and then lay on his side, his head resting on his bent elbow. Still coughing and retching, he struggled to turn over and sit up.

'Don't suppose you got any dry tobacco?' he said.

Comfort reached into his pocket and produced his pouch of Bull Durham. It was wrapped in oilskin and although it was soggy, it seemed to have survived. Together, they rolled a couple of limp looking cigarettes. Only after they had done so did they realize that they had nothing to light them with.

'Hell, just how far are we from shore?' Bannock said.

Comfort's eyes were adjusted to the darkness and he could see that there was only a narrow stretch of water between themselves and the nearest shoreline. The banks appeared to be quite steep and he was just trying to calculate the likeliest spot for them to get ashore when his thoughts were interrupted by a movement behind the recumbent form of the oldster. He had heard no sound, nothing like a splash, but the next instant there was a dull muffled noise like footsteps and something glistened in the moonlight. Bannock uttered a shout and with surprising energy leaped to his feet. He wasn't a moment too soon. The next moment a pair of gaping jaws snapped shut where his head had just been. Comfort, realizing that they were under attack by an alligator, reached for his six-gun, but when he pulled the trigger the wet gun failed to fire. Instantly he flung it at the head of the alligator which, ignoring the oldster, turned its attention to Comfort.

With unexpected speed it slithered forward, its head held high and its jaws opened wide. Comfort could smell the rancid odour of its mouth. He leaped to one side and as the alligator slithered by, turned and flung himself on top of it. It was an instinctive reaction and he had no idea what he was going to do next. The alligator continued its forward momentum and the next moment Comfort felt the water slide over him. He realized that he was in danger of being dragged under and fell away into the water. The alligator turned as Comfort struggled back to the sandbank. The alligator was splashing now as it came up behind him and Comfort thought his time was up.

Although his back was turned he sensed that the gaping jaws and razor-sharp teeth were about to slice him when he saw Bannock skip forward with a knife in his hand. As the alligator's jaws closed he jammed the knife between them, wedging it there so the blade sank into the roof of its mouth. Comfort felt liquid spurt on his back; he didn't know whether it was blood or water and he didn't take any time to find out. Together, he and Bannock scrambled to the far end of the sandbank where they turned, expecting the alligator to come after them. Instead, the creature stood for a few moments, only its tail moving, then, as quickly and suddenly as it had arrived, it turned and slipped into the black waters.

Its two erstwhile victims watched it vanish into the darkness, then turned and looked apprehensively about them, expecting the alligator to emerge again and continue its attack. Every ripple carried a sinister overtone of dread and fear but nothing happened. The alligator, at least temporarily, seemed to have gone. They looked at each other.

'D'you reckon that critter's on Wilder's payroll as well?' the oldster queried.

Comfort looked across the river.

'Hell, I wonder what else might be lurkin' in there,' he said.

'I don't fancy waitin' to find out,' Bannock replied.

They both regarded the narrow strip of water between themselves and the shore.

'Me either,' Comfort said, 'but what are we goin' to do about gettin' across?'

The oldster thought for a moment.

'I guess we ain't got no choice. We just got to chance it,' he replied.

They stood on the edge of the sandbank, hesitating to go back into the water.

'It ain't far,' Comfort said. 'Do you think you can make it?' A sudden thought struck him. 'Hell, can you even swim?'

The oldster gave a faint grin. 'Reckon I can now,' he replied.

Despite the desperateness of their situation, Comfort couldn't help breaking into a laugh.

'Well, now's the time to find out,' he said. 'Try and stay close to me.'

With a look at each other, they took off their boots and, holding them over their heads, stepped into the water, being careful not to make a splash which might attract the alligator or another of its kind. After a few steps Comfort stumbled and fell face forwards into the water. He had been expecting to have to swim but although the riverbed shelved downwards, it was only slight. They moved forward. They couldn't help but make some splashing. The water began to rise but it reached no higher than their waists.

The shore was getting near but both men's nerves were stretched and they looked anxiously about them for signs of an alligator. At times they each felt something slither between their legs and Comfort stepped on something soft which made him flinch. Their clothes were having a dragging effect and progress was slow. The bank was quite high but at one point it seemed to have crumbled and they directed their course to that point. There were rocks and stones beneath their feet and they both kept stumbling but the water was now no higher than their knees and with another few steps they were out of the water and staggering up the river bank. The stones gave way to mud and it wasn't easy to grope their way up. The earth was soft and muddy and they both slipped back but, clutching at anything which might give them purchase, they succeeded at last in reaching the top.

They sat down on the grass to get their breath back and then pulled on their boots. Although they were wet and exhausted, their overwhelming sensation was one of relief. They looked over the dark expanse of the river. The paddle steamer had long disappeared and the only dim light was the buoy which marked the sandbank.

'Well,' Bannock said. 'It weren't quite the boat trip I was envisagin'. Don't reckon I'll be takin' another in a hurry.'

Comfort suddenly found himself thinking of Corrina Stead. Would she miss his presence on the boat?

'There ain't much point in lyin' about here,' he said. 'I reckon we'd best get movin'.'

The oldster coughed. 'I could sure do with a drink,' he said.

'Have you any idea where we are?' Comfort replied.

'Yeah, I think so.'

'Must be a long haul to Cayuse Landin'.'

'We don't need to go all the way to Cayuse Landin'. Besides, we're wanted men there, remember.'

'So what you got in mind?'

'Like I said, I got a shack. It's still a long ways, but it's closer and safer than Cayuse Landin'. It ain't much, but it'll seem like a palace after this.'

Comfort rose to his feet. The first glimmerings of dawn were touching the sky.

'OK,' he said. 'Let's get started.'

The oldster stood up. He bent down, coughed and spluttered once more, then drew himself upright.

'This way,' he said.

They began to walk. The coming of dawn brought with it a chilling breeze and they both felt miserable in their sodden clothes. Comfort began to think about the reason for having ridden the paddle boat in the first place and his first conclusion was that it had been a waste of time. At least they had come out of it in one piece. Then he found his thoughts reverting again to Corrina Stead. His meditations were interrupted when Bannock touched his arm.

'Listen!' he said.

Comfort stopped. At first he could hear nothing other than the lapping of water but then a shift in the direction of the breeze brought the unmistakable sound of hoofbeats.

'Could be anybody,' he said.

'Yeah, and it could be some more of Wilder's boys.'

They stepped back into the sheltering cottonwoods lining the riverbank. Comfort was beginning to be irritated by Wilder. Whenever he tried to concentrate his attention on finding Briggs, the rancher seemed to crop up.

'I forgot to thank you for what you did back there with that alligator,' he said. 'Come to think of it, that's the second time I've had to say thanks for comin' to my assistance.'

'Hell, you saved my life when you jumped into the water after me,' the oldster responded. 'It's me should be thankin' you.'

'What exactly happened to you?' Comfort said.

'I don't know. I came out of the saloon to look for you. Next thing I knew someone had come up behind me and hoisted me clear over the rail. Took me completely by surprise.'

Comfort quickly told him about his fracas with the man who had accosted Corrina.

'It had to be him. He must have realized you were with me and figured it was an easy way to get his revenge. Goldurn it, I probably even put the idea into his mind when I said I ought to have chucked him overboard.'

The sound of horses was drawing closer and they both melted back into the cover of the trees, from where they were able to peer out and see a considerable distance down the track. They could now hear the rattle of wheels and then a wagon came into view, pulled by two straining horses. It was partly covered and going very slowly.

'What the hell is that?' Comfort breathed.

A smile wreathed the oldster's mouth.

'Unless I'm very mistaken, that's the Reverend Bent,' he replied.

Comfort gave him a puzzled look.

'He travels about in that old wagon. Expect he's done a meetin' in Cayuse Landing and is on his way to Willow. He's headed in that direction.'

'He's up and about mighty early,' Comfort replied.

'Sure. He'll have camped someplace overnight.'

Comfort still looked unconvinced.

'Don't worry. He might preach fire and brimstone, but he's OK.'

The wagon took a turn in the trail, revealing some writing scrawled on its canvas side:

Repent Your Ungodly Ways. The Hour Is Nigh

'Hey,' Bannock said. 'We're in luck. The reverend knows me. We've both been around a long time. We could hitch us a ride in the wagon.'

'I hope you're sure about this,' Comfort said.

Without waiting to explain matters further, Bannock stepped out of the trees and stood on the track. Comfort followed close behind. There was no change in the progress of the wagon. It lumbered on at the same plodding pace.

'Howdy, Reverend!' Bannock called.

The reverend raised his whip by way of answer and then, coming close, drew the wagon to a halt.

'Is that you, Bannock? Seems like you're a long ways from anywhere. Where's your hoss? And who's that with you?'

'Ain't got no hoss. We took us a ride on the paddle boat. Had to get off kinda early, you might say.' He turned to Comfort. 'This here is a good friend of mine. Reverend Bent, meet Mr Will Comfort.'

They exchanged nods. For the first time Comfort took notice of the new arrival. He looked to be about sixty and was as gaunt as a rail. He wore a chimney-pot hat and a long dark coat, and under his chin curled a long tuft of beard that made him look like a billy-goat.

41

'Looks to me like you folks could do with a ride,' the reverend said.

'I'm glad you said that,' Bannock replied.

'Hop right in. If I didn't know better, I'd say you been givin' yourselves an early baptisin' in the river.'

'Yeah, somethin' like that.'

Comfort and Bannock went to the back of the wagon. The canvas cover was partly unfolded and they hoisted themselves over the tailboard. The reverend gave a low word of encouragement to the horses, accompanied by a kind of click with his tongue, and the wagon lumbered forward.

'You forgot to ask where he's goin',' Comfort said.

'Who cares? I'm just about all in. Like I said, he'll be headin' for Willow.'

Comfort laid his head back. Bannock was right. What did it matter where they were going? A welcome languor induced by the steady plodding of the horses and the swaying of the wagon began to overcome him.

'I don't suppose we'll be passin' anywhere near this shack of yours?' he said, rousing himself for a moment.

'Nope. Wrong direction.'

There was silence till a loud droning noise started up and filled the wagon. The oldster was snoring and before long Comfort's eyelids drooped and they were both asleep.

CHAPTER THREE

Rank Wilder sat his horse and surveyed the scene before him. Just about as far as the eye could reach was his property. His cattle grazed the best grass in the country. He ran the town of Cayuse Landing and more or less controlled traffic on the river. He had a lot to lose and he didn't intend taking any chances. He ruled by fear and intimidation and he knew he couldn't allow anything to interfere with that. If the townsfolk ever got the nerve to consider rebelling, it could threaten the entire structure he had built up. So when he heard about the killing of three of his best boys, including the Drewitt brothers, he was more concerned than might have been expected. If someone – anyone – stood up to him, he had to be removed. He turned to his foreman, a hardcase named Kilter.

'You sure that no-good rodent Bannock was involved?' he said.

'So it seems.'

'I can't believe it. What could have got into the old goat?'

'Sure seems strange. Maybe he'd been drinkin'.'

'If so, it didn't affect his shootin'.'

He paused and continued to look about him.

'Have the boys found either of them yet?' he asked.

'There ain't been no sign of 'em. You want me to get the marshal to round up a posse?'

'Nope. You say Bannock has a shack somewhere?'

'Yeah. It's near the river somewhere between Cayuse Landing and Willow.'

'There's a good chance they'll make for it. Take a few of the boys and ride out there. Wait and see if they turn up.'

'What if they don't?'

'Burn it out. But give 'em a day or two first.'

'Sure.'

Kilter made to ride off. 'By the way, I been puttin' the word out on the river,' he said.

'Good. I want Bannock and this other *hombre* eliminated.'

Kilter applied his spurs and his horse broke into a trot. Wilder watched him and then turned towards Cayuse Landing. He felt in need of the services of one of Miss Annie's girls. Maybe more than one.

Comfort woke feeling stiff and sore. His head ached. He looked round for the oldster but there was no sign of him. The wagon had stopped. Slowly, he got to his feet and peered out. He was cheered by the sight of a fire just beginning to blaze and the Reverend Bent placing slices of bacon in a pan. He looked up as Comfort dropped from the wagon.

'Hope you slept well,' he said. 'Figured you two could do with a bite to eat. Git your clothes dry too.'

'Sure sounds good,' Comfort replied. 'Where is Bannock?'

Almost by way of reply, the oldster appeared from round a corner of the wagon carrying a blackened pot.

'Water for coffee,' he said. He placed it over the flames. 'How are you feelin'?' he asked.

'Like I been in a fight with an alligator,' Comfort replied.

The oldster chuckled. 'Ain't nothin' to what Wilder's likely to have in store. For both of us.'

The reverend looked up.

'You boys been upsettin' Rank Wilder?' he said.

'It ain't difficult,' Bannock replied.

'That man ain't got no religion,' the reverend said. 'He's a wolf that needs tamin'.'

Comfort sat down beside the fire. Soon the warmth began to work its effect on him and his clothes started to dry.

'I sure appreciate this,' he said, 'but if this Wilder is all you say he is, you might not want to get involved.'

Bent did not reply. Instead he concentrated his attention on the bacon. He heated up a can of beans and soon they were enjoying a good meal. Comfort felt just about dried out and as they drank their coffee he began to feel like a regular human being again. Bannock seemed to have recovered too. The only thing Comfort felt was missing was a good smoke. As they relaxed, the reverend seemed to take up the conversation where it had been left off.

'You were sayin' somethin' about Wilder. What you done to upset him?'

'It's a bit complicated,' Comfort said.

'Guess it must be to get old Beaver here involved.'

The oldster grinned. 'Guess you're more used to seein' me about the Crystal Arcade,' he replied.

'Reckon we owe you an explanation,' Comfort said. Quickly, he regaled the reverend with a brief account of what had happened on the boat.

'I heard somethin' about what happened to the Drewitt boys,' the reverend responded. 'Now that wouldn't have been you two, would it?'

'Those Drewitts were just lookin' for trouble,' Comfort said.

'I ain't holdin' no brief for Wilder or his gang,' Bent replied. He looked thoughtful. 'What was the name of this man you're lookin' for?' he said.

'Briggs,' Comfort replied. 'Lonnie Briggs. Why, you heard the name?'

The reverend's brows were creased in concentration.

'Yeah,' he said at length. 'I think I have.'

Eagerness lit up Comfort's face more than the flames of the fire.

'Where?' he said. 'Some place around here?'

'There was a meetin',' Bent replied. 'It was near a place called Greenoak.'

'I know of it,' Bannock intervened. 'It's downriver in the swamp country.'

'It weren't much of a meetin' but some folks got up and gave their testimony. One of 'em mentioned his name. I didn't take much notice at the time but now

46

you've brought it up, I reckon it might have been Briggs.'

Comfort leaned forward and refilled his coffee cup.

'Don't sound like the sort of thing Briggs would get up to,' he said. 'Beggin' your pardon an' all.'

'The wind bloweth where it listeth,' the reverend responded.

'Can you remember what he looked like?'

Bent shook his head. 'Nope. Can't remember a thing about him.'

'I guess that wouldn't be surprisin',' Comfort said. 'There weren't anythin' particularly distinctive about him.'

The reverend ran his goat's beard through his fingers, twisting it as he did so.

'I do remember one thing he said,' he remarked.

Comfort looked at him over the rim of his cup.

'He mentioned a place called Jaspersville. That struck me because if it's the same place I'm thinkin' of, it's down in Georgia. I spent a lot of time that way when I was a youngster before the war.'

Comfort looked up and exchanged glances with Bannock.

'Yeah,' he said. 'It's down in Georgia. I spent some time there too.'

The reverend didn't respond. If he had caught any significance in Comfort's words, he did not register it. Instead he got to his feet and tossed the dregs of his coffee to the ground.

'Time we was movin',' he said. 'I don't know what you fellas intend doin'. I could take you all the way to

Willow if you want.'

'We need guns and horses,' Comfort said.

'That ain't all,' Bannock responded. 'I could sure do with a change of clothes and a drink.' He looked sheepishly at Bent. 'Just a small one,' he added.

'OK,' Comfort said. 'We'll take you up on your offer, Reverend, and be mighty grateful for the opportunity.'

They doused the fire and put their utensils back in the wagon. This time Comfort sat up on the wagon box beside the reverend and Bannock took up a position just behind them. The reverend urged the horses to take the strain, clicking again with his tongue, and they were on their way. Comfort was working on what they would do after they got to Willow but there wasn't much doubt in his mind. The oldster must have been thinking along similar lines. Presently his voice piped up.

'I guess I know what we're gonna do next.'

'Yeah,' Comfort said. 'What's that?'

'Ride on down to Greenoak.'

'You ain't wrong,' Comfort replied.

They didn't wait around in Willow, only taking long enough to do what was necessary. After paying a visit to the bath-house and purchasing some clothes, they called in at the gun store and picked themselves a couple of Winchester rifles and four Colt Army .44s with ammunition. Lastly they bought horses, bay and dun geldings. As they rode out, they passed the reverend, who had set up camp where they had left him just outside of town. Having already said *adios*, they didn't stop but waved in acknowledgement. The reverend watched them till they dwindled in the distance. Then he spat and, poking about underneath the wagon seat, pulled out a half-full bottle of Forty-Rod. He took a swig and then sat down to rest his back against a wagon wheel before taking a second and a third.

'Sure was lucky coming on the reverend,' Bannock remarked.

'Yeah. We owe him,' Comfort replied.

They rode steadily, for the most part roughly paralleling the banks of the river, allowing the horses to go at their own pace. After their recent experiences, they felt restored. After a time Bannock slowed and Comfort did likewise.

'Problem with your hoss?' Comfort said.

'Nope. Was just thinkin',' Bannock replied.

'What about?'

'A few miles further down the trail and we'll be passin' close to my old shack.'

'You wanna stop by?' Comfort said.

'We got a long ride to Greenoak. I know we picked up a few supplies in Willow, but I'm thinkin' it might not be a bad idea to stock up. I got some vittles and some medicines might come in useful.'

'Makes sense if it ain't too far off the track,' Comfort replied.

They decided to swing by the oldster's cabin. After a few more miles they took a turn-off. A little further on a shallow stream joined the trail and ran alongside. Presently Bannock held up his hand as a signal for them to stop.

'You thinkin' what I'm thinkin'?' Comfort said.

'Someone's been ridin' here recently,' the oldster replied.

'Yeah, I thought I saw sign too.'

They both slid from leather and examined the ground. It wasn't hard to discern the imprint of horses' hoofs and when they walked a little way along the stream they found places where the banks had been disturbed.

'How many do you reckon?' Comfort said. 'I figure three or four.'

'Yeah, that's what I think.'

'Maybe it don't mean anythin'.'

'Maybe not, but the cabin is kinda secluded. Don't tend to get a lot of visitors.'

'There's only one way to find out,' Comfort replied.

They remounted and continued riding, but before long Bannock again gave the signal to halt. They got down and tethered the horses.

'Best go the rest of the way on foot,' Bannock said.

They took their rifles and stepped forwards. Before they had taken many paces they had their first view of the shack through some intervening brush. It wasn't much of a place, made from rough-hewn logs and roofed with sod. It sagged in the middle and the remains of a veranda were pitted with holes. Behind it stood a broken-down corral. From where they stood, they could see no horses but the oldster's keen eyes picked out traces of where they had been.

'Somebody's been here. They've made an effort to sweep the place and cover their tracks.'

'If they've hidden their horses someplace close by, it can only mean they don't want anyone to know they're there.'

'And that means they ain't up to no good,' Bannock said. 'I don't like nobody takin' over my cabin. I figure we're just gonna have to do somethin' about the situation.'

'Is there a back door?' Comfort asked.

'Nope. Only one way in and out.'

'Question is, are they there now?'

For a time they contented themselves with watching the cabin closely but it wasn't giving away any of its secrets.

'They must be waitin' for me to show up,' Bannock said.

'More likely they'll be hopin' it's the two of us.'

'You think Wilder's involved?'

'Either way, why disappoint them?'

Bannock thought about it for a few moments.

'You wait here,' he said. 'I'll go back, get my horse and then ride on in. They'll have to show their hand.'

'You'll be takin' a hell of a risk. Assumin' they're in there, they might just shoot and no questions asked.'

'It's a possibility, but on the other hand they won't be expectin' any trouble. They think they've covered their tracks here but they weren't too clever about leavin' sign further along the trail. They're more likely to let me ride straight in. If I know Wilder's boys, they'll enjoy having some fun at my expense. Besides, they'll want to try and find out where you are.'

'We could just turn and ride away,' Comfort said.

He saw the look on the oldster's face.

'Just posin' all the options,' he added.

'Stay out of sight. Keep me covered when I ride in.'

The oldster slipped away and Comfort took up a position where he had a clear view of the shack. A few minutes passed, then he heard the clatter of hoofs as Bannock approached on the bay. He rode past Comfort without a glance and then emerged from the cover of the trees into the open space in front of the shack. Almost immediately the door flew open and two men emerged.

'Well, if it ain't Bannock!' one of them said. 'What took you so long? We been expectin' you.'

Bannock climbed down from the saddle as a third man appeared from inside the shack.

'Take his horse round to the corral,' the first man said.

The newcomer stepped off the broken veranda and took Bannock's horse. Bannock hadn't spoken but now he turned to the man who had been doing the talking.

'What are you doin' here, Kilter?' he said.

'Well, that ain't friendly,' Kilter replied.

Suddenly his hand dropped to his gun. At the same moment Bannock drew his .44 and in the exchange of fire that ensued Kilter staggered backwards, blood pouring from his chest. The other man's gun was in his hand but before he could fire at the oldster, Comfort's Winchester spat flame and lead and he went crashing into a stanchion before hitting the edge of the veranda, where he lay still. Comfort ran forward as a shot rang out from inside the house. It was a wild shot and before the person could repeat it Bannock had fired through the doorway. There was a grunt and the sound of a chair being toppled.

Comfort didn't wait to follow the action but carried on sprinting round the side of the shack. He was met by a burst of gunfire and bullets kicked up the ground in front of him. The gunnie there had let go of Bannock's horse which was moving sideways and whinnying with fear. Comfort zigzagged as the man began to run. He was gaining on Comfort when there was another burst of fire from inside the house and the man flung up his arms and fell forward, hitting the ground with a resounding thud. Comfort drew up in surprise. Two more shots rang out and then there was silence. Comfort wasn't sure what had happened. He started to move towards the front of the shack when Bannock's voice called out.

'You OK, Comfort!'

'Yeah! How about you?'

'I'm OK. I got a graze to the shoulder but it's nothin' much.'

There were footsteps within the shack, then Bannock appeared round the corner.

'Those three are dead,' he said.

Comfort moved quickly but cautiously to where the fourth gunman lay. It only took a glance to show him that he was dead too.

'What happened?' Comfort said as Bannock came up behind him. 'I didn't shoot him.'

'Me either. The varmint in the shack shot him through a window. He must have panicked and assumed he was you or some other *hombre* on the opposite side.'

'You figure that's all of 'em?'

The oldster nodded. 'We'll find their horses hidden somewhere among the trees,' he added.

They went inside the shack. The place was in a mess but there was no serious damage – other than that which had already existed. Comfort took a good look at the place.

'How long you been livin' here?' he said.

'Can't remember. A long time.'

The oldster seemed to consider the question before turning again to Comfort.

'Come on,' he said. 'We'll bury these varmints and then get back on the trail.'

By the time they had finished the unpleasant task it was late in the day.

'Suppose we stay on,' Comfort said. 'Ride on first thing tomorrow.'

The oldster shrugged.

'Stay if you like,' he said. 'I guess it's possible we could be visited by some more of Wilder's gunslicks.'

'I don't think so. Leastways not just yet.'

The oldster stood on a piece of the veranda. A mist was coming up from the stream. From round the back of the building a horse whinnied. They had put the gunslicks' horses in the corral.

'What do we do with them?' the oldster asked.

'Strip their saddles and turn 'em loose. They'll find their way to where they belong. If they don't, somebody'll come across 'em.'

'Let's do it,' Bannock replied.

'There ain't no rush.'

'Let's do it. We'll give 'em a good feed and set 'em loose. Then let's get goin'.'

The oldster moved away. Comfort watched him till he vanished around the corner of the shack.

'Now I wonder what's eatin' him,' he said to himself.

The sun was low on the horizon when they rode out. It wasn't a time Comfort would have chosen but the oldster hadn't changed his mind about wanting to be off. They took two of Wilder's horses as pack animals and loaded stuff from the shack on to them. Apart from that, Comfort reflected, it wouldn't be a bad idea to have a change of mounts.

At about the same time, Miss Annie was sitting in her room at the Crystal Arcade. There was a knock on the door.

'Who is it?' she shouted.

'It's me, Jenny', a faltering voice replied.

'Wait a moment.'

Miss Annie got to her feet and without thinking glanced at herself in the mirror. It had become second nature to her. Then she moved to the door and opened it.

'Come on in,' she said.

She motioned to a settee and was about to take a nearby chair when she saw that Jenny was crying. Instead, she sat down next to her and put her arm round Jenny's shoulder.

'What is it?' she said.

The younger woman put her head on Miss Annie's shoulder. Miss Annie waited for a few moments before gently raising her head.

'This is not like you,' she said. 'Come on, you know you can talk to me.'

Jenny was sobbing and tears coursed down her cheeks. Miss Annie gave her a handkerchief and then got to her feet. She took a bottle from a cabinet, poured two drinks and, taking one herself, handed the other to the weeping girl.

'Go on,' she said. 'It'll do you good.'

The girl took a sip and Miss Annie sat down beside her again.

'Now, tell me what the trouble is.'

Jenny took another sip and then, making an effort to control herself, began to speak in broken syllables.

'It's Mr Wilder,' she said.

Annie opened her mouth to say something, then changed her mind. She waited for Jenny to resume.

'I know I shouldn't complain. You took me in and I'm making a good living. I don't have any problems with the other customers but I don't think I can see Mr Wilder again.'

Annie waited.

'At first it wasn't too bad but now. . . . He wants me to do things I don't like.'

Miss Annie took a sip of her brandy.

'I tried. . . . At first it wasn't too bad. There were just little things. But now. . . .'

She began to cry once more. Miss Annie took her in her arms and placed her head against her shoulder.

'It's all right,' she said. 'You don't have to say any more. I will have a word with Mr Wilder. You won't need to see him again.'

Jenny sat up with a sudden jerk. 'Please don't say anything to him,' she said. 'I don't know. . . .'

'Don't worry. I won't refer to anything that's been mentioned here.'

'But what if . . . Mr Wilder won't like. . . .'

'Ssh. Don't bother you pretty head about this any more.'

Miss Annie looked down at her protégée.

'Why not take a few days off?' she said. 'Have you anywhere to go? Is there anybody you would like to see?'

Jenny shook her head.

'You can spend a few days at my house,' Miss Annie said. 'There's plenty of room. It'll do you good to have a rest.'

'That would be nice,' Jenny sobbed.

'Just forget about all this business with Mr Wilder. I understand how you feel, but believe me, it'll be just a storm in a teacup.'

Jenny made to get up.

'No need to rush off,' Miss Annie said. 'Stay for a while, until you feel better. In fact, if you wait here, I'll walk back with you when I'm finished.'

When she was satisfied that Jenny was OK, Miss Annie finished her drink and went out, locking the door behind her. The sounds of merriment from downstairs grew louder, and as she began to descend the stairs she smoothed her dress and tidied her hair in readiness to play her role as hostess. She wasn't surprised at what Jenny had told her. It wasn't the first time she'd heard complaints about Wilder. She was just a little concerned that he seemed to be getting worse as time went by and she wasn't sure how much longer she could continue to pacify him.

Comfort and Bannock rode through a changing landscape of pine woods and cypress swamps. Huge live oaks spread their limbs, draped with moss, across the trail. Above the reedy marshes rose islands of sharp-edged sawgrass. When night fell they slept in their blankets on the nearest patch of higher ground to a swelling chorus of frogs and the elusive eerie glimmerings of will-o'-the-wisps. A dank, earthy smell hung in the warm, humid air.

'I hope the reverend was right,' Comfort said as they approached the town of Greenoak.

'Are you sure this whole thing ain't one big wild-goose chase?' Bannock replied.

'Guess we'll find out soon.'

Shortly after bypassing Cayuse Landing they had caught up with the paddle steamer making its way down the river. Comfort caught himself straining his eyes for a possible sight of Corrina Stead before he realized how ridiculously he was behaving. Now he had put his thoughts of her behind him.

It was late afternoon when they rode into Greenoak. The town was small, with a narrow, tree-lined main street.

'If Briggs is here, he should be easy to find,' Comfort remarked.

They made their way to the nearest saloon and tied their horses to the hitch rail. As they stepped through the batwing doors Comfort was already looking about him, seeking for the remembered face. The place was quiet, with only a few men sitting at tables and a little knot of idlers gathered about the bar.

'Whiskey?' the bartender queried.

Comfort nodded. The barman poured and looked the newcomers up and down.

'Just rode in?' he queried.

'Yup.'

Comfort and Bannock took their drinks and retired to a table set against the wall. Comfort observed the customers more closely. They presented the usual motley group. Occasionally one or other of them would glance across at the new arrivals. After a time the batwings swung and a small white-haired man wearing a tin star came through. He nodded towards the group at the bar and then, glancing at Comfort and Bannock, made his way to their table. Comfort nodded.

'Howdy,' he said.

The marshal took a seat beside them.

'Have a drink?' Bannock said.

The marshal shook his head. 'Saw you boys ride in,' he said. 'Seein' you with those packhorses made me think you've maybe come a long ways.'

'Ain't no law against that,' Comfort said.

'Sure. I ain't questionin' your right to be here. I just like to introduce myself to anyone new in town. Sort of get acquainted.'

'Well, it's sure nice to have met you.'

The marshal seemed to relax. A smile spread across his features.

'So, you wouldn't mind me askin' what brings you here?'

Comfort exchanged glances with Bannock. He could see no reason not to answer the marshal's question with the bare truth.

'I'm lookin' for a man called Briggs,' he said.

He thought he detected a slight movement of the marshal's countenance.

'Briggs,' the marshal repeated. 'Can I ask why you want to find this man?'

'Sure. He's an old friend. I heard he was seen down this way.'

The marshal looked closely into Comfort's face. Bannock, looking up towards the bar, noticed that some of the men were taking an interest.

'Have you heard of him?' Bannock said. 'Greenoak seems a tight little place. I would guess you have a pretty good knowledge of what goes on around here.'

The marshal paused. He gave Comfort and Bannock the benefit of another hard look.

'OK,' he said. 'Yes. I've heard of Briggs. In fact, right now he's sittin' in one of my cells. If it's the same fella, that is.'

Comfort swallowed the last of his whiskey.

'What's he doin' in jail?' he asked.

'Drunk, disorderly, disturbin' the peace. Nothin' too serious.'

'Can I see him?'

The marshal thought for a moment. Again, a smile

raised a corner of his mouth.

'Yeah, sure,' he said. 'In fact, you might be able to do me a favour by bailin' him out.'

'OK. If it's the man I'm lookin' for, I'll take him off your hands.'

The marshal got to his feet. 'Come on, then,' he said.

He walked away, Comfort and Bannock following. The street outside was deserted; a few lights had sprung up which only seemed to add to a sense of solitude. They walked down the street, the jangling of their spurs emphasizing the oppressive quiet. The marshal's office wasn't far and when he opened the door a man sitting inside with his legs on a table got rapidly to his feet.

'Any problems with the prisoner?' the marshal asked.

'Nope. He finished his food and I took away the tray.'

The marshal nodded in the direction of Comfort and Bannock.

'These gentlemen think they might know him. They're willin' to take him off our hands.'

The marshal reached into a drawer of a desk and produced a set of keys. He went through a door at the back of the room, indicating to the others to follow. Comfort was feeling nervous and agitated but did a good job of keeping his feelings in check. It was dark in the narrow corridor behind the door and it took a few moments for their eyes to adjust. There were two cells. One of them was empty; in the other a man sat on an iron bedframe with his head in his hands. He didn't look up at their approach and only did so when the marshal addressed him.

'Briggs, you got visitors.'

He raised his head. Comfort came close, peering through the bars. The man inside was unshaved and his lank hair hung almost to his shoulders. He was thin to the point of emaciation and Comfort felt a sense of disappointment. His first reaction was that this couldn't be the man he was looking for. Briggs in turn was looking at him closely.

His mouth opened. Slowly, he struggled to his feet and approached closer. In his eyes was a dawning light of recognition.

'Comfort,' he said. 'Is it you?'

Comfort was suddenly animated. It wasn't so much the man's look which awakened a dawning sense of recognition, but the timbre of his voice.

'Briggs,' he said. 'I been lookin' for you.'

The marshal stepped forward and unlocked the door.

'You can go now,' he said. He turned to Comfort. 'See my deputy about the paperwork. I don't know what you boys are plannin' to do, but I'd just as soon you left town. I ain't sayin' you ain't upright citizens and all. Let's just say I don't want to have to put it to the test.'

Comfort wasn't prepared to argue, especially since he had found the man he was looking for. He had no intention of remaining long in Greenoak.

Once they had settled matters with the deputy, they saddled up one of the packhorses. Briggs was already looking better than when they had found him. Now Comfort could discern the features of his former comrade in the prison camp. He had changed a lot but beneath marks of time and change the lineaments of

62

yesteryear were beginning to emerge.

It was dark when they rode out of town. Comfort's main aim was to find somewhere to camp where they could make themselves comfortable and he could talk with Briggs. He would have preferred to book in at the hotel but he wasn't in any mood to risk putting the marshal's back up. Before they had been riding long Bannock found a suitable spot. When they had eaten and settled down to enjoy a pot of thick black coffee, Briggs produced a pouch of tobacco and offered it to the others.

'Guess I ought to thank you two for gettin' me out of jail,' he said.

Although he had seemed quite comfortable with his new situation, it was the first time he had had a chance to speak. They rolled cigarettes and lay back in the warm glow of the camp-fire.

'It weren't nothin',' said Comfort. 'The marshal said you were in there for bein' drunk and causin' a nuisance. Is that right?'

'Yeah. It ain't somethin' I'm proud of. Truth is, I been hittin' some hard times. I let things get to me. I tell you what, though. I sure never expected you to come by and rescue me.'

'It wasn't an accident. Like I said in the jailhouse, I been lookin' for you.'

Comfort looked closely at his old comrade. 'Hell, it's been a long time. What you been doin' with yourself?'

Briggs blew out a ring of smoke. 'This and that,' he said. 'Just lately I been gettin' by huntin' muskrats.'

Bannock had noticed some weathered cabins built

on piles among the marshes. He had been puzzled as to what they could be. Now he understood; they were the dwellings of muskrat hunters.

'There's plenty of the critters around here. You probably saw their houses, kinda like yellow anthills. Yup, this is good muskrat country.'

He paused, enjoying the taste of the tobacco, and seeming to almost relish his musings.

'Good muskrat country,' he repeated. 'Guess they like those cattails.'

He took a sip from his hot coffee mug and it had the effect of jerkng him out of his reverie.

'You said you were lookin' for me,' he said to Comfort. 'What were you lookin' for me for?'

Now that Briggs was touching on the main issue, Comfort suddenly felt awkward. He didn't know where to begin his tale.

'Remember Jaspersville?' he said.

Briggs was silent. He inhaled deeply, then swallowed a mouthful of steaming coffee so quickly that he spluttered.

'Remember Laidler?' Comfort continued. 'You and me swore we'd get revenge on the skunk. We arranged to meet, but I never made it.'

Briggs turned his head to stare at Comfort. 'I was there. What happened to you?'

'Like I say, I couldn't make it. I was ill. Really ill. I was lucky to pull through.'

'I waited for you. Waited for two days.'

'You didn't do anythin' about Laidler?'

Briggs shook his head. 'No, I didn't do anythin''

64

about Laidler.'

He sat up and flicked the stub of his cigarette into the flames. 'Is that what all this is about? After all this time, you've come searchin' for me because of Laidler?'

'Yeah. I just regret not makin' it the first time. I guess I let you down pretty bad.'

Suddenly Briggs broke into a laugh.

'Laidler!' he said. 'Hell, that was so long ago. He's probably dead by now!'

'If he ain't, he will be when I get my hands on him.'

Briggs's laughter grew louder. 'Are you crazy?' he said.

'I ain't crazy. That varmint's not gonna get away with the way he treated us. He's gonna pay.'

Briggs's laughter subsided. He pulled out his tobacco pouch and began to build another smoke. He passed the pouch to Bannock.

'You know about this?' he asked him.

Bannock nodded. 'Yeah.'

'And you went along with it?'

'There are other reasons why we're ridin' together.'

'By Jiminy, I hope there are.'

Briggs addressed himself to Comfort once more. 'Do you know where Laidler is? Assumin' he's alive.'

'No. That's why I'm here. I figured we'd look for Laidler together. It shouldn't be too hard to find him.'

'And you want to make him pay. Look, I ain't tryin' to defend Laidler. He was just about the worst type of low-down evil coyote. But take a look at me. My life ain't been the same since Jaspersville. I admit it. I ain't been able to get it back on track. But I ain't plannin' on bringin' it all back up again. Findin' Laidler and killin' him ain't gonna bring back those wasted years and it ain't gonna give me some kind of release.'

'You sayin' you're not interested in trackin' Laidler down? If that's the case, why did you swear that oath?'

'We were different people then. Sure, I meant it at the time. If you'd have showed up that first time I'd have gone through with it. But I ain't the same man I was then. Too many things have happened.'

Bannock had remained largely silent. Now he spoke to Comfort.

'I think Briggs is right,' he said, 'although I can't speak for you boys. My experiences in the war were different. But look at it this way. We were on opposite sides then. Hell, we might have been slinging lead at one another on some battlefield. But that was then, not now. The war's over and gone. Maybe it's time you let it go.' Comfort sprang to his feet.

'You're wrong,' he said. 'You're both wrong. What's a man worth if he goes back on his word?'

The oldster shook his head ruefully.

'You tellin' us you ain't ever changed your mind?' he muttered.

'Changin' your mind is one thing. This is somethin' plumb different.'

Comfort rounded on Briggs. 'OK. Go back to your muskrats. Go back to Greenoak and get drunk and wind up back in jail. What the hell do I care?' He turned to face the oldster.

'Same goes for you. If you don't want to ride with me, go back to Cayuse Landing. Go back to the Crystal

Arcade and start swampin' the place.'

'You don't mean that,' Bannock replied. 'You know that ain't what I was implyin'.'

Comfort stood for a moment regarding the others in the dancing light of the fire. Then he turned on his heel and walked away. A few moments later they heard the sound of creaking leather and then the soft muffled sounds of hoofs. They had a fleeting glimpse of a dark shape riding away into the darkness. Briggs got to his feet and made to move towards the horses.

'Let him go,' Bannock said.

'I didn't mean to—'

'I know. Me neither. But it ain't gonna do nobody no good to carry this on. He'll see things different soon enough.'

'Maybe he's got reason.'

'Yeah, reckon he has. But so have you.'

Briggs hesitated and then resumed his place by the fire.

'Maybe things will look different in the mornin',' Bannock said. 'I reckon the best thing we can do is get some sleep.'

CHAPTER FOUR

Corrina Stead and her brother Daniel got off the boat at Tidesville. Standing on the quay, waiting to meet them, was a tall, angular man with a white beard, wearing a frock coat-and a panama hat.

'Uncle Winslow!' Corrina cried on catching sight of him. 'Uncle Winslow!'

She waved her arms and he came forward to enfold her in a warm embrace. Then he shook hands with Daniel and, after seizing one of the cases with which Daniel had once again been engaged in a struggle, led the way to a Dearborn which stood nearby with its canvas sides pulled back. Once everyone was installed and the luggage hoisted on board, he took his seat and flicked the reins. The street was busy but the light-weight carriage weaved its way deftly through the crowds of people and traffic. From somewhere beyond the main street of the town a band was playing and, glancing to her left, Corrina had a glimpse of a field of tents and streaming flags.

'Ain't seen the place so busy in a long time,' Uncle

Winslow remarked.

'How have you been keepin'?' Daniel asked.

'Seein' you two has made me feel a lot better,' Uncle Winslow replied.

'And Aunt Lucinda?'

'She's fine.'

They had passed beyond the town limits and were driving through a rich countryside studded with farms. They turned up a tree-lined track which presently led under a sign reading LAZY ACRE and then, round a slight bend in the road, the farm-house emerged. It was a small, white-painted building set among locust trees with a flaking barn behind it, and a well. In front the yard was kept clean but off to the side a number of chickens scuttled about in the mud and a few pigs squealed in a pen.

'Oh, I love this place,' Corrina cried.

On the porch of the house an elderly lady wearing a purple taffeta dress and with her hair drawn tight in a bun appeared; as the Dearborn stopped she rushed forward.

'Corrina!' she cried. 'And Daniel. It does my eyes good to see you.'

As soon as they had stepped from the coach, Corrina and her brother were ushered into the house. A youngster of about eighteen appeared from the direction of the barn.

'Harlin, take charge of the horse. See she gets a good feed,' Uncle Winslow said. 'When you've put the wagon away, bring the luggage up to the house.'

'Sure, Mr Clayburne.'

Clayburne patted the horse and then went inside. His wife was already serving coffee with some biscuits and cakes she had made.

'When we've had a chance to chat,' she said, 'I'll take you up to your rooms. Lords-a-mercy, I swear you two have grown.'

Corrina laughed. 'I hope not, Aunty,' she said. 'I'm nearly twenty now and I hope I'm full growed.' She turned to her brother. 'And he's not far behind.'

'I'm sure you make a fine young man and a fine young woman. Don't you think so, Winslow?'

'Your father must be plumb proud of you both,' replied Uncle Winslow.

'When you've finished, I'll show you to your rooms, and then I wouldn't mind bettin' you'll be wantin' to get on down to the fair.'

Corrina grinned and nodded her head.

'If you don't mind us rushin' straight off.'

'Of course not. That's just what we figured.'

'We got a couple of horses saddled up and waitin',' Uncle Winslow said. 'Figured you might appreciate a ride.'

'Are you not comin?' Daniel asked.

'Not this time. Thought I'd leave you two young folks to enjoy yourselves.'

'And I'll have a good hot meal waitin' for you when you get back. With flapjacks for supper.'

Corrina put her cup down and went over to squeeze her aunt.

'Now just you go easy on an old lady,' said Lucinda.

There was a knock on the door.

'Come on in,' Winslow shouted.

The door opened and Harlin came in with the cases.

'Here, I'll take them now,' Daniel said.

Together, they hoisted the cases upstairs. Corrina and her aunt followed behind. Neither Corrina nor her brother needed to be shown their rooms. They had been there before and Corrina knew just what to expect. There were flowers in vases and a beautiful patchwork quilt lay across the bed. New curtains fluttered in the slight breeze from the partly opened window.

'It's lovely,' Corrina said.

'I'll leave you to make yourself comfortable,' Aunt Lucinda said.

When she had gone Corrina sat at the dressing-table and looked at herself in the mirror. Her face was flushed and she felt excited, but there was something else written on her features. She found herself thinking again of the man who had come to her rescue on the boat. Not for the first time she recalled his blue eyes. There was something about him, but she didn't know what. She had not seen him again. That was strange. Hadn't he said that he was getting off at Tidesville? She suddenly thought it would have been nice to introduce him to her uncle. But why? She had barely met him. She realized with regret that she didn't even know his name.

Her thoughts moved on. She had seen nothing, either, of her molester. She suddenly shivered. The incident had upset her more than she had thought. Unwillingly, she began to wonder what had become of him too. What if he had got off the boat at Tidesville? But then surely she would have noticed. She was being foolish. It had been a minor incident and she shouldn't be giving it more significance than it warranted. Should she have told her brother? On the whole, she was glad she hadn't.

She picked up a comb, and began to brush her hair; presently she was comforted by the sounds of her brother moving in the next room. She started to think about the fair. They would both enjoy the ride to town.

After galloping out of camp, Comfort headed for the trail leading back towards Greenoak. The town was asleep. Not a light showed as he passed close by. He was feeling bitter and angry and didn't have any plan in mind other than to head back to Cayuse Landing. He rode hard for a while until common sense returned sufficiently for him to realize that he was pushing the horse too hard; he slowed down first to a canter and then to a walk. He had a long way to go. His brain was a welter of thoughts and impressions. Daylight came and he rode on. About mid-morning he drew rein and slid from the saddle. He set the horse to graze while he built himself a smoke.

So Briggs was out of the game. What did it matter? He would find Laidler himself. He had let Briggs down once. That made it all the more incumbent upon him to do things right now. He finished the cigarette and rolled another. He felt calmer and the faint sounds of the river rolling away off to his right reached his ears with a soothing murmur.

His eyelids felt heavy and they were beginning to close when he thought he heard another sound. Instantly he was alert, listening closely. At first he could hear nothing and thought he must be mistaken when it came again – the sound of approaching hoofbeats. Quickly he was on his feet. He moved to the horse, took hold of the reins and led it to the shelter of some trees. Then he withdrew the Winchester from its scabbard and, after glancing about him and taking stock of the landscape, secreted himself behind a clump of bushes.

The sounds of galloping hoofs grew steadily louder. He reckoned there were at least two horsemen. Maybe they were just a couple of riders passing harmlessly along the trail, but his recent experiences with Wilder and his men had made him more careful. Presently the riders came into view, coming towards him along the trail he had been riding. He was right; there were two of them, one slightly in front of the other who was leading an extra horse. He was looking at the ground and Comfort had a sudden conviction that they were following his sign. He hefted the rifle. Could Wilder have found out already what had happened to his boys at Bannock's shack and got on to their trail so quickly? It seemed very unlikely.

Then he reflected that if they were two of Wilder's gunnies, they were coming from the wrong direction. They seemed to have slowed down and it was taking them an age to cover the remaining distance. The sun was getting warm and a slight miasma, rising from the river, seemed to hang in the air. They were getting closer and he raised the rifle in readiness. For a moment he held it to his shoulder, then he put it down again. He had recognized the two riders. They were Bannock and Briggs. For a moment he considered letting them ride by but as they came almost abreast of his position, he stepped out from the trees. Bannock was in front. Instinctively his hand went towards his gun, then he recognized Comfort. He reined in his horse and Briggs did likewise.

'What took you so long?' Comfort said.

'You son of a gun, you could have got yourself killed.'

'I'd say it was the other way round,' Comfort replied. 'It's plumb lucky for you I ain't one of Wilder's boys.'

Bannock slid from the saddle. 'Funny you should say that,' he said.

Behind them, Briggs dismounted and walked forward.

'What do you mean?' Comfort asked.

'We figured it was just possible you might have stayed in town, so we rode through. The marshal wasn't too pleased to see us.'

'He was up and about plumb early,' observed Comfort.

'There'd been trouble. Some cowboys hit town and caused a rumpus. Him and his deputy got things calmed down. They persuaded the troublemakers to leave town but they figured they'd best wait around. I figure he didn't get any sleep last night,' Bannock told him.

'What's this got to do with me?'

'The marshal took a look at their horses. They were carryin' a Lazy Acre brand. The Lazy Acre is near

74

Tidesville. Could be horse rustlin' is another one of Wilder's sidelines.'

'Wilder again. Greenoak is a long ways from Wilder's spread. I wonder what they were doin' this far south?'

'That's what the marshal was wonderin' too. He's heard plenty about Wilder and even had a brush with some of his riders before.'

'Why did he tell you this?' Comfort asked.

The oldster shrugged. 'He didn't exactly say so, but I reckon he maybe thought we had somethin' to do with it.'

'He didn't mince his words,' Briggs said. 'He made it mighty clear he don't want to see any of us again.'

'Yeah,' Bannock concluded. 'He didn't exactly invite us to stay around for breakfast.'

'There's an idea,' Comfort said. 'Have you folks eaten this mornin'?'

'Nope. Got straight on your tail.'

'Me neither and I'm sure beginnin' to feel hungry.'

'What about Wilder's boys?' Bannock said.

Comfort turned and looked at him.

'You figure they're after us? If so, they haven't wasted any time.'

'I been thinkin' it over and I don't think there's a connection. I don't see how they could have got down here so quick.'

'How many were there?'

'Three.'

'I don't see it either,' Comfort said. 'Still, if they're around some place, we'd better be on the watch.'

Bannock licked his lips. 'Sure could put away some

grub,' he said.

They set about preparing breakfast. While they did so, they remained silent. Comfort was feeling awkward. So far nobody had referred to the previous night's dispute and Comfort felt he had behaved badly. After they had eaten and were putting away a mug or two of thick black coffee, he turned to Briggs.

'I reckon I owe you an apology,' he said. 'Guess I just kinda got too worked up about things.'

'Hell, no need to apologize,' Briggs said.

'I don't agree with what you said and I still intend lookin' for Laidler, but I got no right to expect you to think the same way as me.'

He turned to Bannock and then back to Briggs. 'And I sure appreciate you takin' the time to come on after me.'

'I'm not certain I thanked you two for gettin' me out of that jail,' Briggs said.

'You almost ended up back inside,' Bannock joked. 'I wouldn't like to face that marshal when he gets really mad.'

'Hell,' Briggs said. 'Seems to me we're getting mighty apologetic. Next thing there'll be an angel choir playin' on their harps if we ain't careful. Isn't it about time we got back on the trail?'

Comfort regarded him doubtfully.

'I been thinkin' too,' Briggs continued. 'Figure I've had about enough of muskrat huntin'. I ain't changed my mind about Laidler, but if you're agreeable, I figure I'd ride along with you. For the time bein' at least.'

Comfort smiled. 'It'd be an honour,' he said. 'Glad

76

to have you along.'

'Which way now?' Bannock said.

'You got a shack standin' empty,' Comfort replied. 'I reckon that's where we head and then take things from there.'

'Sounds good to me,' the oldster responded. 'After all, you didn't get much of a chance to get acquainted with the place last time.'

It was late. Miss Annie and Jenny had not long returned from the Crystal Arcade and Annie was making a snack for them to eat before turning in for the night. Since living with Annie, Jenny seemed to have recovered something of her old self. It helped that nothing had been seen of Wilder since the day his treatment of Jenny had led to Annie taking her in.

'Would you like coffee?' Annie called.

'No. Better not,' Jenny replied.

Annie looked out of the window. Behind the kitchen garden lay a small stretch of grass backed by a fence, on the other side of which was a broad alley with a barn facing it. Beyond the barn was open country with a rough track leading eventually to the river. The kitchen was quite dark, only the light of a lamp providing illumination, and as she peered out she thought she saw something moving.

She opened the back door, moved to the fence and leaned on it. She could hear muffled hoofbeats and as her eyes grew accustomed to the darkness, she discerned a couple of riders coming along the track. It was but little used, since the best way to the river was through the town, and she was immediately suspicious. She turned away, went quickly back inside and doused the lamp. She paused for a moment, wondering what to say to the girl that wouldn't scare her, but there was no time for hesitancy. The riders were approaching fast. She went through the door into the living room and turned down the lamps there too.

'What's happening?' Jenny said.

'Probably nothing, but there's two men approaching through the meadow and it don't hurt to be careful.'

'Two men?' Jenny immediately became agitated. 'You don't think. . . ?'

'I don't think anything. Go upstairs.'

'What about you?'

'Don't waste time. Just go upstairs and keep out of sight.'

Jenny rose to her feet and rushed to the stairs. She slipped as she ran up them but quickly recovered. Annie heard the door of Jenny's room close. Quickly, she reached into a drawer and took a derringer which she placed in a pocket of her dress. Then she glided to the window and peered out.

The prospect was empty and deserted. She withdrew behind the curtains but after a moment held them back a fraction to look out again. Still no sign of anybody. Suddenly she jumped at a loud rapping on the back door. She stood against the wall. The rapping was repeated. She realized that she was holding her breath, as if anyone outside could hear the slightest suggestion of a sound. There was a pause and she was beginning to hope that whoever it was had decided to go away when there came a loud thud followed by a second and a third. She realized that someone was attempting to kick the door down. If she had had any doubts about the intentions of the riders, she had none now. Whoever they were, they were out for trouble. The kicking at the door continued and the door began to splinter. She realized that there was no point now in hiding. She needed to be bold and do something. With a glance towards the ceiling, she moved forward and turned up the lamp.

'Who is it?' she called. 'Hold on, I'm coming.'

She took the lamp in her hand and walked through the door into the kitchen as another kick shook the door.

'Stop that!' she called. 'I'm opening the door.'

She put the lamp down and fumbled at the bolt. The door was badly splintered and wouldn't survive another couple of kicks anyway. She drew the bolt and before she could do or say anything, the door flew open and two men advanced inside. Despite the dim light, she recognized one of them as one of Wilder's boys, a regular at the Crystal Arcade, named Carl Sabin. Neither of them had spoken so far.

'What is the meaning of this?' she said.

The men smelt of drink and stale tobacco.

'Sabin, answer me. Just what do you think you're doing?'

She was standing in front of Sabin. By way of reply he swung his arm, sweeping her aside. Followed by the other man, he clattered through into the living room.

'Where's Jenny?' he said.

79

'Jenny? If she's not at the Crystal Arcade, I don't know where she is. I don't see what business it is of yours, either.'

'It's Mr Wilder's business. He wants Jenny and he wants her now.'

'I don't understand what you're talking about.' Annie was trying desperately to think of something which might deter the intruders. 'There are other girls. Why would Mr Wilder be wanting Jenny?'

Sabin shrugged.

'Come on,' he said to the other man. 'She's got to be upstairs.'

As the men moved to the foot of the stairs, Annie darted forward and stood in their way.

'I tell you, she's not here.'

'We know she is. We know you been hidin' her.'

Sabin swung his fist and hit Annie in the mouth. She felt blood ooze out as she fell backwards on the stair. Sabin was already past her when she drew the derringer, but before she could fire it the other man had kicked it out of her hand. He picked it up and stamped past her. She made a desperate grab for his leg and he shook it in an effort to escape her clutch. Grimly she held on as she heard a thud from upstairs followed by the sound of splintering wood and then a shrill scream.

'Leave me go, you bitch!' the man snarled.

At the same time he raised the derringer and brought it crashing down on Annie's head. She let go her grasp as a wave of pain and nausea enveloped her. She heard another scream from upstairs and then the sounds of a scuffle. Her attacker had reached the head of the stairs. Summoning her remaining strength, Annie began to climb the stairs. Before she had reached the top the men emerged carrying Jenny who was screaming and kicking her legs. Sabin's boot swung and Miss Annie's head jolted back as she went tumbling down the stairs. She lay at the bottom in a crumpled heap as the men brushed past her. She heard the back door slam and then the sound of horses galloping away into the night. She began to struggle to her feet as a black tide swept over her and she was no longer conscious of anything.

Even before he arrived at his shack, Bannock sensed that something was wrong.

'How do you mean?' Briggs asked.

Bannock tapped his stomach.

'I can feel it here,' he said. 'It's just a kinda extry sense.'

'More like that meat an' gravy you cooked up last night,' Comfort replied.

All the way up they had been on the lookout for any of Wilder's boys, but they had seen nothing of them and Comfort, for one, was fairly convinced that their presence in Greenoak had been coincidental. Bannock agreed but when he mentioned it to Briggs he seemed curiously non-committal.

When they arrived at the clearing all Bannock's forebodings were justified. Nothing remained of the shack but a burned-out ruin. The oldster got down from his horse, and poked about among piles of scarred wood and cinders. As he kicked his way through the mess, clouds of ash rose like ghosts of the dead building.

'Guess I had it comin',' he said. 'I coulda guessed that when Wilder found out what happened to the Drewitts, he wouldn't wait around to get his revenge.'

'I'm real sorry,' Comfort said.

'The more I see and hear of this Wilder *hombre*, the less I like him,' Briggs muttered.

'It don't matter,' Bannock said. 'That shack never amounted to a hill of beans. I can build another.'

They looked about them. There were still traces of hoofprints and some dried-out droppings.

'What do we do now?' Bannock asked.

Comfort had been doing some quick thinking. On the way up from Greenoak they had passed close by the town of Tidesville and Comfort had felt a quickening of the pulse. His rational self told him that there was no chance of seeing Corrina Stead, but the mere fact that she was associated in his imagination with the settlement was enough to create that strange frisson of expectation. He found himself thinking of the occasion of their meeting when they had boarded the river boat. That had been at Willow, which was the next town from Bannock's shack. They had also passed near Cayuse Landing. He had been tempted to look up Miss Annie but that could wait. At some point, he thought, he might either pay a visit to Tidesville or continue to Willow. But either of those options would have to wait too.

'Ain't much we can do right now,' Comfort said. 'We been doin' a lot of ridin'. This ain't what we expected, but I guess it's as good a spot as any to set up camp.'

'Sorry I can't offer you boys somethin' better in the way of hospitality,' Bannock commented.

Late that evening, having attended to the horses and eaten, they sat around the campfire. The night was full of sounds; the rippling of the stream, the soughing of the wind in the treetops, the hoot of an owl. Suddenly a new sound insinuated itself into Bannock's ears and he sat up.

'What is it?' Comfort said.

'Can't make it out. Sounds like wheels.'

'I can't hear anything,' Briggs said.

Comfort listened carefully before addressing Bannock.

'Me neither,' he said. 'For an oldster, you got pretty sharp ears.'

'There! That was surely a horse.'

'What? Do you reckon it's Wilder's boys again?'

Briggs was on his feet, his six-gun in his hand. Comfort reached for his rifle. They were both surprised to see a broad grin spread itself across the oldster's face. Somehow, his front teeth looked especially prominent.

'No need to get excited,' he said. 'Unless I'm way wrong, that's the sound of the Reverend Bent's wagon.'

Briggs still looked apprehensive but he was persuaded to put his gun away. They waited while the sounds grew louder so that they all could hear them. After a time a dark shape lumbered into sight and the sound of a voice rang out.

'Ho there! I come in peace.'

'Howdy, Reverend,' Bannock called back.

The wagon came close, stopping just outside the

circle of light cast by the flames, and the Reverend Bent stepped down.

'Figured it might be you,' he said to Bannock. 'A mighty shame about your cabin.'

'Come and join us,' Bannock said. 'You know Mr Comfort. Let me introduce another friend: Mr Briggs.'

Briggs and the reverend shook hands.

'Briggs,' the reverend repeated. 'Would this be the Mr Briggs I mentioned to you?'

'The very same,' Comfort said.

Briggs looked confused.

'It was the reverend who put us in the way of findin' you,' Comfort explained.

'In that case, I'm in your debt,' Briggs observed. 'If it hadn't been for these two, I'd be in jail right now.'

'Ah! Are we not enjoined to set the prisoner free?'

'I don't know about that, but it sure worked in this case.'

Comfort, who was watching closely, thought Bent looked particularly closely at Briggs. He opened his mouth as though to say something more, but if he had been about to speak, he was prevented by an interruption from the oldster.

'I figure you could use some coffee?'

The reverend turned away from Briggs.

'I'd be obliged.' Bent made a difficult job of sitting down. 'Rheumatism,' he said. 'My own thorn in the flesh. In this case, the knees.'

He stretched his legs out.

'The flesh is weak,' he commented.

'What are you doin' here, Reverend?' Bannock said.

'About the Lord's work, as always. What does the Good Book say? Take nothing for the journey but a staff only.'

Bannock handed him a cup of coffee. The reverend swallowed a mouthful and spluttered.

'That sure tastes good,' he said.

For a moment they lapsed into silence, then Comfort offered the reverend his pouch of tobacco. When Bent had built a smoke he lit it from the fire.

'Have you any idea what happened here?' Comfort said.

The reverend shook his head.

'Last time I came by, it was still standin'. But it don't make no difference whether I saw anythin' or not. We all know who done it.'

'You mean Wilder?'

'I understood you boys were already runnin' from him, the first time I met you.'

'We weren't runnin',' Comfort said.

'Mr Comfort has other business,' Bannock added.

Comfort looked at him, wondering whether there was a hint of facetiousness in his comment.

'Would that be the same business made him seek out Mr Briggs?' the reverend enquired.

Comfort leaned forward and topped up his cup of coffee. He offered to do the same for Bent.

'That's good coffee,' the reverend repeated.

Comfort put the battered coffee pot back on its tripod over the flames. As he did so he observed that Briggs was sitting forward, looking towards Bent with apparent interest.

'That was a fine meetin', Reverend,' he said. 'The one I was at down Greenoak way. I got to say your words really affected me.'

'Hallelujah!' Bent said. 'Not all the seed falls on stony ground.'

'You found religion?' Comfort asked.

'I found that it weren't worth wastin' any more time on the likes of Laidler.'

At the mention of Laidler the reverend suddenly sat up.

'Laidler,' he said. 'Did you say Laidler?'

Comfort turned to him. 'Does the name mean somethin' to you?'

The reverend seemed to draw back.

'You told me somethin' of your business when I picked you up after you come ashore from that boat. Maybe you'd better fill me in with the rest of the story.'

Comfort nodded and turned to Briggs. 'You got any objection?'

Briggs shook his head. 'Like I say, it don't mean anythin' to me now.'

Without elaborating, Comfort outlined the events in which he and Briggs had been involved in the War Between the States. When he stopped, he allowed time for the reverend to assimilate what he had said.

'You gave the impression the name Laidler meant somethin' to you,' he observed at length. 'Is that right?'

The reverend paused, giving Comfort a searching look.

'Just outside of Tidesville there's a farm called the Lazy Acre. It's run by a fella called Clayburne, Winslow

Clayburne. Only that ain't his full name. His full name is Winslow Laidlaw Clayburne.'

Briggs looked across at Comfort. 'It don't mean nothin',' he said.

'Maybe I've said too much,' Bent continued. 'Clayburne is a good man. I've knowed him a long time. He ain't the type to be runnin' no prisoner-of-war camp. Like Briggs says, it don't mean nothin'. It's just a coincidence.'

'Seek and you shall find,' Comfort remarked.

'Yes, and the devil can quote Scripture,' Bent replied.

Suddenly Comfort recalled Bannock's words about the brand the marshal had observed on the horses of the men who had caused trouble in Greenoak.

'He said it was a Lazy Acre brand. We assumed Wilder had rustled 'em. What if it wasn't Wilder at all but this man Clayburne?'

'I'm gettin' way confused,' Bannock said. 'I know Winslow Clayburne too, and I can confirm what the reverend says. Winslow Clayburne is a good man. He's well respected round Tidesville.'

Briggs leaned forward. The flickering flames only served to emphasize the intensity of his features.

'If I'm gettin' this right,' he said, 'that would mean Clayburne was probably not lookin' for you at all. More likely, he was lookin' for me.'

Comfort's gaze was firm on his old comrade's features.

'Yeah. And it's my guess is that he was doin' that because somehow he got wind that you were lookin' for him.'

87

Briggs returned Comfort's steady look without flinching but didn't reply.

'It was no accident you bein' in these parts, was it?' Comfort continued. 'I found you here because you'd traced Laidler to Tidesville. You knew Clayburne and Laidler were one and the same.'

Bannock and the reverend were watching with close attention. The fire had burned down but it suddenly flared and hissed as the flames ran along a sappy branch. A nerve twitched in Briggs's cheek.

'I didn't know for sure,' he said. 'Not until now. I guess that business in Greenoak just about clinched it.'

'You just said it meant nothin', Clayburne's middle name bein' Laidler. You know that's not true.'

'It don't mean nothin' to me no more. And even now, I ain't completely convinced.'

'You were holdin' back on me,' Comfort said.

'Nobody's holdin' out on nobody,' the voice of Bannock suddenly cut in. As if by way of support, Bent spoke.

'Maybe I spoke out of turn. I certainly didn't intend . . .'

'It's OK, Reverend,' Briggs said. He turned back to Comfort.

'It was somethin' the reverend said at the meetin'. It kinda spoke to me, made me start thinkin'. Maybe it just brought somethin' out into the open, somethin' that had been botherin' me, holdin' me back. I guess that was why I stayed downriver: to try and work it all out.'

'Is that so?' Comfort replied. 'So what was it the reverend said that was so important?'

'I can't remember exactly. He was quotin' Scripture. Somethin' about not gettin' angry, not lettin' bitterness rule your life.'

' "Cease from anger and forsake wrath; fret not thyself in any wise to do evil",' the reverend interposed.

Comfort glanced at Bannock. In the dancing fire-light he had the impression that the oldster's head was nodding.

'You can think as much as you want,' he said to Briggs. 'I'm takin' a ride to this Lazy Acre to see for myself if Clayburne is the man we're lookin' for. I'm not restin' till I've put things to rights.'

CHAPTER FIVE

Once they had installed themselves Corrina and her brother mounted the horses which had been put at their disposal and set off on the road to town. It wasn't. far but they both appreciated the ride. As they approached Tidesville they could hear the sounds of music floating on the air and the approaches to the town were a busy scene of passing rigs and excited people dressed in their best clothes for the occasion. The county fair was a big event in the district.

Tethering their horses to a hitch rack on the outskirts of the field on which most of the activities were centred, they made their way through the crowds of people jostling around the tents and stalls which had been set up. They passed by various exhibitions of produce and artefacts made by local people, stopping to glance at coconut shies, boxing booths, shooting galleries, ten-pin alleys and all kinds of other attractions, till they came to some pig and cattle pens. A sale of horses was taking place and a large number of people were taking part in the bidding. Corrina's eyes swept the crowd. She was excited and vivacious and she was looking out for anybody she might know. Suddenly her eyes fixed on a face in the crowd and she flinched. The face was grinning back at her with leering eyes. It was the man who had accosted her on the boat. Noticing the change in her demeanour, her brother looked at her.

'Somethin' wrong?' he asked. 'You look like you seen a ghost.'

She made an effort to collect herself.

'Sorry. Let's move on,' she said.

'But I ain't finished here,' Daniel retorted. Then, seeing that his sister was unhappy about something, he took her arm and they moved away. As they walked Corrina couldn't help glancing behind her.

'Something's happened to upset you,' Daniel said.

She turned back. 'It's nothing,' she replied.

Seeing that he still looked puzzled, she thought it best to give a brief account of what had happened on the boat.

'And you say the man's here, at the fair?'

'I don't think I was mistaken.'

Daniel stopped. 'Come back with me,' he said. 'I'll deal with him.'

'No, no; it's better to just leave it. I'm sure I'm making a fuss over nothing. It was only a minor incident. I shouldn't be making so much of it.'

They walked a little further. Daniel noticed for the first time that his sister was trembling.

'We've seen most things,' he said. 'Would you like to go back? We can always return tomorrow.'

She looked up at him with shining eyes. 'Are you sure you wouldn't mind? I wouldn't like to spoil things for you.'

'We've had a busy day,' he replied. 'I reckon we've both had enough for now.'

They made their way back to where they had left the horses. Every so often Corrina glanced over her shoulder but she had no further sight of her molester. They mounted and made their way at a steady pace through the crowds and back along the main street of town. Soon they were on the road leading back towards the Lazy Acre. Once they were clear of the last of the holidaymakers Corrina began to relax.

'I'm sorry,' she said. 'I'm sure you would have liked to stay in town a little longer.'

'Nonsense,' he replied. 'Besides, we got days to spend.'

Suddenly his comments were cut short by the bark of a rifle. Still looking at his sister with a disbelieving expression, Daniel slid slowly from the saddle. As he hit the ground Corrina screamed once and then dropped down beside him.

'Daniel!' she said. 'Daniel, speak to me!'

A trickle of blood was issuing from his mouth but otherwise she could not see any wound. She looked about and then her heart sank. A rider was bearing down on her and she knew at once that it was the man from the boat. He must have followed them as they left the fair, then got ahead and waited in ambush. She rose to her feet and moved back towards her horse but the rider was already upon her. Drawing his horse to a sudden halt, he leaped down and before she had time to do anything to prevent him, seized her roughly by the shoulders. She had a terrifying vision of his evil face as he forced his lips on hers. He smelt badly and her gorge rose. His hands were clawing at her dress and she heard it rip. She tried to scream again but he clapped his hand over her mouth.

'You thought you could get away from me,' he hissed. 'Well, your boyfriend ain't around to help you this time.'

She tried to speak but his hand was too tight around her mouth.

'Nope, I've dealt with him. Come on now: don't pretend you ain't likin' this.'

The hand over her mouth slipped slightly and she sank her teeth into his palm.

'You dirty bitch!' he shouted.

His hand swung and caught her a heavy blow which knocked her to the ground. In an instant he was on top of her, his hands clawing at her garments. She still struggled but it was hopeless. The man was too strong for her and she had just about given up when, through the pain and the horror she heard the sound of hoof-beats. The next moment the man was hauled from her.

She didn't know what was happening. She managed to sit up, gulping great draughts of air, then she glanced around. Two men were holding her attacker and a third was laying into him mercilessly with his fists. The man groaned, hanging limply as blow after blow was delivered to his face and stomach. His features were an indistinguishable mass of blood and bone. She looked closely at the three men who were delivering the punishment and recognized them as some of her uncle's men. One of them was Harlin. A horse snickered nearby and the sound seemed to give one of the men an idea.

'OK, tie him to one of the horses and drag him.'

It only took a matter of moments till it was done. Only then did the sense of what was happening register with Corrina.

'No,' she cried. 'That's enough.'

Either the men didn't hear her or they were too intent on meting out the punishment they felt their victim deserved. Ignoring her, they slapped the horse's rump and it started to move. One of them whipped out a gun and fired into the air while Harlin waved his hat. The frightened horse began to gallop. The men were whooping as the figure of the man who had attacked her was dragged face down over the rough earth. Only when the horses had charged a considerable way did Harlin seem to remember Corrina and run to her side.

'Miss Corrina,' he said. 'Are you hurt?'

Gathering her tattered garments about her, Corrina shook her head.

'I'll be OK,' she managed to say, 'but please see to my brother.'

As if he had noticed Daniel for the first time, Harlin sprang to his side. He kneeled down and raised Daniel's head. Then he rose to his feet.

'He's hurt but I don't think it's bad.'

He ran to one of the horses and came back with a canteen from which he poured water over Daniel's face.

To Corrina's huge relief, Daniel's eyes flickered and then opened. Harlin held the canteen to his lips and he took a few sips. Corrina began to sob.

'Better get him back to the Lazy Acre,' Harlin said.

She was about to reply when she was brought up short by a sudden burst of gunfire. She looked up. One of the Lazy Acre men was standing over the body of the dragged man with smoke issuing from the muzzle of his revolver. Corrina shuddered.

'He won't be troublin' you again, ma'am,' Harlin said.

Corrina stood for a few moments rooted in horror and disbelief, trying to make sense of what she had just witnessed. Although she was hurt herself and shaking with the terror of what the man had done to her, she couldn't believe the outcome. Even more powerful than the feelings evoked by the attack on her was the shock and revulsion she felt at what had happened to the culprit. It didn't seem credible. She knew these men and Harlin especially. She had always thought of him as a good boy. He was just an ordinary young man who worked on her uncle's farm. Whenever she had encountered the other two, they had always been pleasant and respectful. She just did not recognize them by their behaviour. At the same time she couldn't help but feel gratitude towards them for rescuing her from a horrible fate and a small part of her even felt glad, telling her the man had deserved it.

'Come on, Mr Stead is losing blood.' Harlin's voice cut into her thoughts. 'You two, help me get him on a horse.'

Daniel was able to assist his helpers in getting him into the saddle. Presently they were on their way. It wasn't far to the Lazy Acre. As she rode Corrina's thoughts and emotions continued to shift and swirl. Amongst them another consideration raised itself, and that was how to reconcile what had occurred with her uncle's kindly demeanour. They were his men. To some extent at least, they took their cue from him. How could that possibly square with life at the Lazy Acre, with her uncle's considerate attitudes, her aunt's gentle concern? A hole seemed to have opened beneath her feet and she had peered into a profound darkness, deeper than the glimpse even her attacker had given her.

Comfort was up before the first rays of dawn, but even so Bannock had beaten him to it. He already had the fire going and a pot of coffee boiling on its tripod.

'Ham and eggs OK?' he said.

Comfort nodded.

'Just as well because we ain't got much else.'

Comfort poured himself a cup of coffee. He glanced over at the recumbent figure of Briggs, who still appeared to be asleep. There was no sign of Bent.

'Where's the reverend?' Comfort asked.

Bannock nodded towards the wagon. Comfort gave it a glance before turning back to Bannock.

'What else do you know about this man Clayburne?' he asked.

'Still thinkin' about him? He's been around awhiles. I bumped into him from time to time. Like I said, he's a good man. Him and his wife run a farm they call the Lazy Acre. They grow soybeans and have a few chickens and pigs. It ain't what you would call a major enterprise but it's big enough for him to employ a few people on a casual basis. They do OK, even though Wilder's been puttin' pressure on some of the farmers around there to sell up.'

'How old is he?'

'I dunno. Somewhere in his fifties, I would guess.'

Comfort nodded his head.

'That would fit,' he said.

'You referrin' to this Laidler *hombre?*'

'Yeah. I reckon he wouldn't have been a lot over forty back in the War.'

The bacon was sizzling in the pan and the sound seemed to arouse Briggs. He sat up and rubbed his eyes.

'Coffee's in the pot,' Bannock called.

Briggs came over and helped himself to a cup. He looked over at Comfort.

'You still figurin' on payin' a vist to Clayburne?' he asked.

'Yeah.'

'Then I'll ride with you.'

Comfort looked his surprise. 'I thought you'd washed your hands of the matter,' he said.

'I think you're doin' the wrong thing, but I'm involved now whatever I think. I only hope some good comes of it all.'

Bannock was shovelling bacon and eggs on to tin plates. As he did so the reverend's face appeared at the opening in the canvas cover.

'Somethin' smells good,' he said.

'Come and join us,' Bannock invited. He turned back to Comfort.

'What Briggs says goes for me too,' he said. 'Just in case you was thinkin' I might be plannin' otherwise.'

'You think I'm wrong about this as well,' Comfort replied. 'Briggs might believe he's still got a part in it, but it never involved you.'

'It involved me the moment I fired my gun and shot Wilder's man. Besides, we done some travellin' together since then and I figure that entitles me.'

They were all silent for a while, tucking into their grub. As they scraped their plates Comfort looked towards the reverend.

'What's your plans?' he asked.

'Me? I was headin' for Cayuse Landin' when I came across you boys. Figure I'll carry right on.'

'We're goin' that way. We'll ride along with you for a whiles.'

'Glad to have your company,' the reverend replied.

Once they had finished eating and doused the fire, they were ready to ride. The reverend climbed to his wagon seat and the others sat their horses. Bannock looked back over the burnt-out ruins of his cabin. He ran his fingers over his stubbled chin, lost in thought for a moment. Then he turned to Comfort.

'What are we waitin' for?' he said.

The reverend's wagon creaked as the wheels began to turn. The other three fell in behind. Alongside the track, the river glinted in the early sunlight.

*

It was obvious to the patrons of the Crystal Arcade that both Miss Annie and Jenny had suffered abuse, and most of the patrons knew at whose hands. They also knew that the same person was responsible for forcing them back when they were so obviously in no state to be on duty. Nobody, however, was prepared to do anything about it, least of all the marshal. Miss Annie's injuries were the more obvious. Her mouth was split, one eye was closed and her cheek was badly bruised. Her scalp was cut and swollen. She had tried speaking to Jenny but the girl seemed to have gone inside herself and did not respond to any of Annie's attempts to communicate. She moved about like an automaton. Mercifully, the clients could not but be aware that something was badly wrong and made no efforts to approach her. Annie saw nothing, either, of Wilder or any of his men. They seemed to have temporarily deserted the Crystal Arcade.

Then, after a week or so had gone by and Annie's wounds were beginning to heal, Jenny disappeared. When she failed to appear in the morning, Annie thought nothing of it. Sometimes the girls overslept or did not feel well. There was little activity in the Crystal Arcade so it was of no consequence. Only as noon approached did she begin to grow concerned. Leaving a little group of drinkers she had been talking with, she climbed the stairs to Jenny's room and knocked gently at the door. There was no response. She knocked again, a little louder, and called:

'Jenny! It's me, Annie.'

She pushed at the door and it opened slightly. She had expected it to be locked. Opening it further, she stepped inside Jenny's room. The place was empty. The bed was a tousled mess and a wardrobe door hung open. The few clothes that it had contained were absent. She stood, puzzled for a moment, but then it was obvious that Jenny had gone. She must have slipped out sometime during the night. Annie moved to the bed, thinking that Jenny might have left a note, but there was no sign of one.

Annie's first thought was that the girl must have run away. Then she remembered what had occurred at her house. Could something similar have happened and could Wilder have taken her again? She tried to recall the events of the previous night but there had been nothing unusual, nothing untoward. If Wilder was responsible, he had been more discreet about it this time. She stood for a while with her head bent in thought. Then she sat down by Jenny's dressing-table and looked in the mirror. Her bruised features looked back at her with a mute appeal. She looked at the reflection of her satin dress and glanced down at it. The image of her mouth drew taut and she stood up.

Quickly now she moved down the corridor to her own room, the one she used when at the Crystal Arcade, and went inside. With sudden energy she undid the fastenings of her dress and stepped out of it. She changed into riding gear and then went quickly down the stairs. A few heads turned as she strode across the room and out through the batwings. Without hesitation she made her way to the gun store and purchased a rifle and a Smith & Wesson .44 six-shot revolver. Then she made her way to the livery stable where she had an arrangement with the ostler to stable her horse and saddled it up.

'Goin' somewhere, Miss Annie?' the ostler said.

'Yeah. Goin' to do somethin' I shoulda done a long time ago.'

The ostler looked puzzled and scratched his head. Miss Annie pulled the girths tight.

'You can tell the boys at the Crystal Arcade I might not be back,' she said.

She led the horse down the runway and climbed into the saddle. Touching her spurs to the horse's flanks, she rode out into the dusty street.

Rank Wilder was sitting in the living room of his ranch house talking with Sabin. On the whole he was feeling pretty good about things. The Black Stirrup was doing fine and he had plans to extend his domain. It wouldn't take a lot of pressure to persuade some of the surrounding farms to sell to him. At the same time, he owned a good part of Cayuse Landing and the town and its marshal were in his pocket. He controlled the flow of river commerce on the Big Muddy.

On a more personal level, he had had his way with Jenny and the girl had been taught a lesson. He had some doubts about Sabin's treatment of Miss Annie but when all was said and done she was only a whore. At times she had shown signs of standing up to him; it wouldn't do any harm for her to be brought to heel and taught the advisability of obedience.

Only one cloud hung like a pennant of smoke from a riverboat funnel on the smooth blue surface of his prospects, and that was the continuing irritant of the oldster Bannock and the stranger he had taken to riding with. His plan to kill them both at Bannock's cabin had failed and more of his own men had died in the process. His foreman, Kilter, had been one of them and that was certainly not good for morale. He had ordered the cabin to be burnt down but Bannock and the stranger still remained unaccounted for. It was only a minor affair, but anything, no matter how small, which challenged his authority was to be ruthlessly resisted. He looked at Sabin over a glass of whiskey.

'This Bent *hombre*,' he said. 'What do we know about him?'

Sabin had a glass of whiskey in one hand and a cheroot in the other.

'I don't know nothin' more than you do, boss,' he replied.

Wilder gave him a quick, piercing look and then drew on his own cigar.

'That ain't the answer I'm wantin',' he said.

Sabin sat up straighter. 'He's got a wagon. He spends his time travellin' up and down the river. He used to hold a lot o' meetin's, hot gospellin', but he don't seem to bother too much now. Folks have kind of got used to him.'

'He's been around a long time.'

Wilder meant it as a statement but Sabin took him up on it.

'I reckon so. A local landmark, I guess you might say.'

Wilder got to his feet and began to pace the floor, talking to himself as much as to Sabin.

'A fella like that, he'd be bound to know what's goin' on. Couldn't be otherwise.' He stopped and turned his attention on Sabin. 'You find this reverend fella and find out from him what's become of that old fool Bannock. I figure he's got to know. And if we locate Bannock, chances are we'll find the other coyote right alongside.'

'What do we do then? I mean, if the reverend tells us where Bannock is?'

'Then you do somethin' about it.'

Sabin still looked a little uncertain.

'Do I need to spell it out? I want those two *hombres* dead. Just make sure there are no mistakes this time.'

Sabin removed the cheroot from his mouth and stubbed it out in an ashtray. He finished off the whiskey and then stood up.

'Who should I take along with me?' he asked.

'I don't care,' Wilder snapped. 'Take who you like. Just don't come back until the job is finished.'

Sabin nodded and went out through the door. On the veranda he paused for a moment. Evening was approaching. A breeze was blowing up from the direction of the river. He spat a gob of phlegm across the yard and began to walk towards the bunkhouse.

Comfort, Bannock and Briggs left the reverend a few miles out of Cayuse Landing, where an intersecting trail would lead them around the town and on towards

103

Tidesville. They watched the reverend's wagon as it continued along the river road till it was obscured by trees, then they swung their horses inland. Bannock took the lead because he was familiar with the route. Comfort and Briggs rode just behind him. None of them spoke as they let the horses go at their own pace. After a time they passed a signpost pointing to Cayuse Landing on their right. Bannock drew his horse to a halt and pointed down the rough trail.

'Someone's come up from there recently,' he said.

He pointed to the ground and as they moved on they could all see clear traces of a rider having continued in the direction they were going.

'Don't mean nothin',' Bannock said. 'Anybody could have come this way.'

'Is it a regular trail?' Comfort asked.

'No. In a little while we'll come to a cut-off. This trail continues in the direction of Tidesville, the other leads towards the Black Stirrup spread.'

'I guess we'll see which way the rider went when we get there,' Briggs commented.

When they reached the cut-off, it was apparent that the sign led in the direction of the Black Stirrup.

'I wonder who would be headin' that way?' Bannock mused.

'Probably some cowpoke goin' back from town.'

'Maybe, but then Wilder's boys usually ride in packs.'

'It don't signify,' Comfort said. 'We got our own business to tend to.'

As they carried on towards Tidesville, Bannock dropped back so that he rode close to Comfort.

'Funny ain't it,' he said.

'What's funny?'

'The way your business became mine and now my business has become yours.'

'I don't get your drift.'

'The Black Stirrup is Wilder's spread. Got me sort of thinkin'. I reckon sooner or later you're gonna have to deal with him.'

'Wilder ain't my priority. That's Laidler.'

'I got a burned-out cabin says Wilder's our real concern now. Not to mention a little matter of bein' thrown into the Big Muddy and nearly eaten by an alligator. Oh yes, and—'

'Shut up,' Comfort said. 'Didn't anybody ever tell you, you talk too much?'

Bannock grinned and moved on ahead. The day was advancing and the sun was growing hot. As they crested a long rise the oldster drew to a halt and pointed off to his right. Looking in that direction, Comfort could see in the distance a glint of water and a hazy suggestion of buildings. He drew out his field glasses and took a look through them. The buildings were those of Cayuse Landing.

'Wonder if the reverend has reached there yet?' he said.

'If he has he ain't likely to stay long,' Bannock replied. 'He sure is a wanderer.'

Comfort turned his head and looked the other way. They had topped a ridge which dropped away on that side into a valley beyond which were some low hills with scattered trees, mainly cedar.

'Wilder's spread starts somewheres beyond those hills,' Bannock said.

'Is that so?' Comfort replied.

He swept the country with his glasses and was about to put them down when he suddenly stiffened. Holding them steady, he peered closely at the scene they revealed. Protruding from behind a bush in the middle distance he saw what looked like part of a leg and a foot. Briggs, waiting for a turn at the glasses, noticed Comfort's intense scrutiny.

'What is it?' he asked.

Comfort handed him the glasses and directed him to the patch of vegetation he had been looking at.

'I don't see nothin',' Briggs said.

'Behind that juniper bush,' Comfort replied. 'Looks to me like a leg.'

Briggs stared hard.

'Hell,' he said at length, 'I think you might be right.'

Bannock looked at them both.

'Let's go take a look,' he said.

Comfort sheathed the glasses and they spurred their horses down the slope. It took them longer to reach the spot than Comfort would have reckoned for but as they approached it was clear that he was right. Extending from the clump of bushes was a leg clad in a riding-boot and above it the hem of a skirt. Reaching the bushes, they jumped from their horses and ran to the spot. The figure of a woman lay stretched out on the grass, face upwards. Comfort flung himself down beside her.

'She's breathin' OK,' he said.

He looked her over for any sign of injury but the only

106

obvious thing he could see was a swelling to her head. Briggs came running up with a canteen of water which he held to her lips. Bannock, who was close behind, took one look at the unconscious woman.

'Jumpin' Jehosaphat,' he said. 'That's Jenny Burns from the Crystal Arcade!'

Just as he spoke the words, her eyes flickered open. She gazed up at them uncomprehendingly before a look of terror and alarm spread across her features.

'Don't hurt me!' she pleaded.

Bannock stepped forward and knelt beside her.

'Miss Jenny,' he soothed, 'It's me, Beaver Bannock. These other people are friends of mine. You don't have anything to fear. We've come to help you.'

Briggs offered her the canteen again and she swallowed some water.

'What happened?' Bannock said. 'What are you doin' here?'

Suddenly tears began to flow from Jenny's eyes and course down her cheeks. She struggled to sit upright and Comfort put his arms around her for support.

'I couldn't let it happen again,' Jenny began to mumble. 'I had to get away. I didn't know what else to do.'

'Let what happen, Miss Jenny?' Bannock said. 'Get away from what?'

'From Wilder. Oh, it was horrible.'

She began to shake with sobs and Comfort held her to his chest until she quieted a little.

'You've got a bump on your head but it ain't too bad,' he said. 'Do you feel pain anywhere else?'

In response she began to weep once more. Comfort looked at the others.

'Guess we'd better take her back to Cayuse Landing,' he said. 'Let the doc take a look at her.'

Jenny began to clutch at him. 'No. Please don't take me back. Don't let Wilder find me.'

Comfort regarded her with a searching look. 'Whatever Wilder's done to you,' he said, 'he ain't gonna be doin' it no more.'

She grew calmer, still cradled in Comfort's arms. Nobody spoke for a while. At length Jenny seemed to have recovered something of her equilibrium.

'Here's what we'll do,' Comfort said. 'You just rest right here, Miss Jenny, while we make things comfortable. I reckon you could do with a cup of coffee and maybe some food inside you. After that, if you feel ready, you can tell us just what's been goin' on.'

'And don't worry none,' Bannock added. 'Like Mr Comfort says, whatever's happened, you're safe now.'

Before long they had built a fire and rustled up some beans and coffee. While Bannock and Comfort were occupied with doing this, Briggs went off and after a time reappeared leading a worn-looking blue roan pony. Jenny looked pleased.

'I'd forgotten about him till now. Thank you, Mr Briggs. It wouldn't have been nice if anything had happened to him.'

By the time she had eaten and put some strong black coffee inside her, Jenny was looking a lot better. Without her having confirmed whether she was carrying any injuries other than the one to her head,

Comfort had pretty well satisfied himself that she was basically OK. Neither he nor any of the others pushed her into telling her story, but eventually she appeared willing to talk. It was obviously still not easy for her to do so and though her account was sparse, it was not difficult for them to read between the lines and fill in some of the details.

'Last night I decided to get away from the Crystal Arcade altogether,' Jenny concluded. 'I got this far and then the horse just took a stumble. He threw me. I must have passed out because that's all I can remember till you found me.'

'That stinkin' varmint Wilder,' Bannock said when she had finished. 'I knew he was no good, but this just about beats all.'

'I'm plumb sorry, ma'am,' Briggs mumbled. 'It just shouldn't be that way.'

Comfort didn't say anything. His mouth was drawn tight and his jaw was clenched.

'You say this man Sabin attacked Miss Annie too,' Bannock asked. 'Was she hurt bad?'

'Sabin hit her. She made out it wasn't serious, but in a way she got the worst of it.'

'You hear that?' Bannock said to Comfort.

Comfort ignored his question.

'That skunk Wilder needs to be dealt with,' Bannock said. 'But then I guess you're still intent on gettin' to the Lazy Acre.'

Comfort looked at the oldster as if he had heard him for the first time.

'Those tracks we saw back along the trail,' he said. 'I

got an idea whose they might be.'

Bannock looked perplexed. 'What are you goin' on about?' he said. 'What have they got to do with anythin'?'

Comfort turned his attention to Jenny.

'Would Miss Annie have missed you this mornin'?' he asked.

'Yes, I suppose so. I usually get up early, like the rest of the girls.'

'You livin' back at the Crystal Arcade?'

'Yes, but Miss Annie has a room there. She don't always stay at her house.'

'What do you think her reaction would be to findin' you gone? Especially after everythin' you just told us.'

'I don't know. I guess she'd get worried and start wondering where I was.'

'Yeah. That's what I reckon.'

'What are you sayin' exactly?' Bannock said.

'Remember, I know Miss Annie. She wouldn't just sit back and do nothin'. She'd start lookin'. And what would be the first place she'd start?'

'The Black Stirrup,' Bannock replied.

'You got it. My guess is that those hoofmarks we saw were made by Miss Annie's horse.'

The oldster whistled. 'By Jiminy, I reckon you could be right,' he said.

Jenny had become agitated at his words. 'Miss Annie will be in real danger if she goes anywhere near the Black Stirrup,' she said.

Comfort leaped to his feet. 'Listen,' he said. 'I'm goin' back to follow those prints. If it's Miss Annie, I'll find her. When Jenny's ready to ride, you two take her back to Cayuse Landing.'

He turned to Jenny.

'Is there some place you could stay? Apart from the Crystal Arcade, I mean.'

Jenny thought for a moment.

'You could stay with the doc,' Bannock said. 'He's a good man. He'll understand the situation.'

'Good,' Comfort said. 'Once Jenny is safe, you two head straight for the Black Stirrup.'

'What about the Lazy Acre?' Bannock asked.

'The Lazy Acre can wait. Right now it's Miss Annie and Jenny we got to concentrate on.'

'And that varmint Wilder,' Bannock muttered between his prominent teeth.

Having come to a decision, Comfort didn't waste any further time. He hoisted himself into the saddle and rode off in the direction from which they had come. When he had topped the long slope he looked back long enough to see the others still gathered about the fire, their distant figures appearing and disappearing against the flames. The day was growing late. He waved his arm and took the trail back towards the Black Stirrup turn-off.

CHAPTER SIX

The Reverend Abraham Bent drove his wagon into Cayuse Landing. He came to a halt in the town square, climbed down and, making his way to the general store, went inside to buy some supplies.

'Howdy, Reverend,' the storekeeper said.

'Howdy.'

'Funny you should turn up. There were some fellas askin' if I'd seen you just yesterday.'

'Yeah? Why would they be askin' you?'

The storekeeper shrugged. 'I guess they knew you call by from time to time to pick up what you need. They probably been askin' other places too.'

The reverend thought quickly.

'What can I be gettin' you?' the storeman said.

Bent moved to the window and looked out on the street. Suddenly his eyes narrowed. Coming down the street were four men he recognized as some of Wilder's boys, and leading the way was Carl Sabin. They passed by the store and, walking a little further, came up to his wagon. They stopped to peer inside. The reverend

112

turned back to the storekeeper.

'Forget those supplies for now,' he said. 'Is there a back way out of here?'

The storeman was hesitant, but then something in the reverend's manner persuaded him.

'Yes,' he replied. 'It's this way.'

He held up a corner of the counter; Bent dipped under and went through a curtained alcove into a store-room. At the back a door stood partly open.

'You ain't seen me,' the reverend said.

Without pausing to explain further, he slipped through into sunlight. The back of the store opened on to a patch of dusty grass beyond which a narrow path led past a few tired looking frame buildings into some trees. Quickly, the reverend made his way down the track and into their shelter, where he stopped to think. Maybe he was being foolish but the combination of the storeman's words and what he had seen through the window of the shop made him suspicious. He had seen something of Sabin and had heard stories about him. If Sabin and the others were looking for him, it meant trouble, and he had already seen what Wilder had done to Bannock's cabin. He had helped Bannock and his friend Comfort, spent time in their company. That in itself would be enough to make him a marked man, if Wilder knew about it.

The more he thought about it, the more convinced he became that Wilder was out to get him. If that was the case, there was only one thing to do. He must throw in his lot with Bannock and Comfort. But there was the question of his wagon. He cursed himself for having driven into Cayuse Landing. He should have followed his first inclination to make camp outside the town. But in that case he wouldn't have been made aware that Sabin was looking for him. He would have been a sitting duck.

He could abandon the wagon, but he was loath to do so. Shadows were gathering around the trees. He looked up at the sky and saw that it was already quite late. He resolved to wait until night had fallen and then attempt to retrieve the wagon. It would be risky. Wilder's men might have the wagon under observation but he doubted it. They wouldn't be bothered to invest the time and patience it would involve. It wasn't their style. They would probably be down at the Crystal Arcade most of the night, getting drunk, confident in their ability to catch up with him at any time now that they knew he was around. He might be wrong. He might have made a bad miscalculation. But he was going to take the chance.

Comfort rode hard until darkness advised caution. The night was dense and he feared he had ridden past the cut-off he had been told led to the Black Stirrup. He continued to look for the faded trail but eventually, realizing he was not likely to find it, he turned his horse and proceeded in what he felt was the general direction. As he rode he went over the events of the day and was surprised at how anxious he felt about Miss Annie. He began to suspect that he might be going the wrong way and wished he had brought Bannock along with him. At least the oldster was familiar with the country.

He came to the conclusion that it might be wiser to wait till the dawn and find the cut-off where he might be able to pick up the lone rider's sign. He began to rehearse all the reasons why it was unlikely that the rider was Miss Annie. It was a hunch but he had nothing better to go by. He knew that there was no point in going on but he was reluctant to stop.

Then, just as he was about to call a halt, he thought he saw a faint glimmer in the distance. It was barely visible at first but as he got a little closer it became obvious to him that it was the glow of a campfire. His pulse quickened. Who would be out on the range at this time of night? He scarcely hoped that it might be Miss Annie. Whoever it was, he needed to take care.

He continued to move forward. At one point the ground dipped and he lost sight of the faint glow but then, as he topped the shallow depression, he saw it again. The night was quiet and sounds carried. He heard the snicker of a horse and then, fearful of his own horse making a noise, drew to a halt and slid from the leather. He hobbled the animal and took off his boots before resuming, walking silently and all the time straining his eyes in order to perceive and avoid any obstacles. The sky was cloudy and it was difficult to see but the fire glow was an unmistakable beacon. When he was close he drew his six-gun in readiness.

Now he could make out a few dim features of the landscape. The fire was built in a hollow, protected on the side away from him by a few bushes where he could just make out the dim shadowy form of a horse. To the side he could discern a vague shape which he guessed

115

was somebody wrapped in a blanket. He took another few steps and then stopped. He was about as close as he dared to go without disturbing either the figure in the blanket or the horse. He was lucky that the wind blew towards him or he might have skittered the horse already. For a moment he hesitated, then he stepped forward boldly, aiming to cover the remaining distance before the person, whoever it was, could react.

He hadn't taken two steps when he felt something catch at his legs and before he could do anything to prevent it, he went tumbling forwards. He hit the ground heavily and his gun was knocked from his grasp. At the same moment he heard the sound of movement behind him and the sharp click of a rifle.

'I got you plumb in my sights,' a voice said, 'so don't try and make a move.'

It was a female voice.

'Annie!' he said. 'It's me. Will Comfort.'

He heard a gasp. 'Turn over so I can see you there.'

He rolled over, his arms spread out. He could now see the woman holding the rifle which was pointed at his chest.

'Will!' she breathed.

At that moment she seemed to wilt and took a step backwards. Comfort was quickly on his feet; he stepped to her side and took her in his arms as she released her hold on the rifle. It clattered to the ground.

'Annie,' he said. 'Thank heaven I found you.'

She looked up at him and in the glow of the fire he could see relief and joy written across her features.

'Will Comfort,' she said. 'You'd be about the last

116

person I'd expect to see out here.'

They parted and Comfort glanced about him.

'Somethin' tripped me,' he said.

'That was my little ruse,' she said. 'I strung a rope across. You must be losin' your grip. I heard you comin' from a way off.'

A grin lit up Comfort's face. 'Hell, I should have known. Annie, you're a hell of a woman.'

'Come and sit by the fire,' Annie said. 'I guess we both got some explainin' to do.'

Comfort continued to regard her. 'I haven't seen you look like this,' he said.

Annie smiled. 'You mean not all painted up and dressed in a satin gown. Hope you ain't disappointed.'

'I sure ain't,' he replied.

Annie broke into a laugh.

'Go get your horse,' she said. 'I'll make some coffee.'

The Reverend Bent waited among the trees, getting more and more restless, till he figured it was late enough to make his break. With a last glance to right and left, he slipped out into the open. From the direction of the town faint sounds of activity in the Crystal Arcade were carried to his ears. Moving quickly, he walked down the narrow track by the deserted buildings and across the open space behind the store. He moved to his left, following the line of the back of the buildings which fronted on to the main street. He came to a passageway and glided down it. As he had anticipated, the alley opened on to the square where he had left the wagon. He had thought it might have been

117

removed by Sabin, but it was still there.

As he looked out he heard footsteps and a figure walked across the square, heading in the direction of the Crystal Arcade which seemed to be the only place still open. He pressed himself against the wall of the building as the figure passed near by and continued along the boardwalk. When it had gone he continued to wait, watching for any indication that the wagon might be under observation. The minutes ticked by. The only thing moving was a cat which wandered slowly across the open space before disappearing round a corner.

Slowly, the reverend moved away from shelter and stepped out into the open, pausing when he had taken a few steps to take another look about him. Faint sounds of laughter floated on the breeze, coming from the Crystal Arcade. To his right he could just make out a hazy glow where the lights from the saloon spilled out from the batwings. He could make out the dim outline of horses tied to the hitch rack.

Satisfied that he was unobserved, he crept forward again, moving quickly and silently. His horses sensed his presence and turned their heads. He heard the slight jangle of their harness. He was up to the wagon now and he paused just for a moment in order to pat the horses' heads. Then, like a shadow, he glided up to the wagon seat and took the reins in his hand.

As he did so he heard, in the shadows of the wagon behind him, the click of a gun being cocked. Instantly his hand dropped to his side and he spun round, firing into the darkness as a roar split his ears and a bullet

went flying past his head. He leaned sideways, firing
again, and heard a gasp of pain. The horses were
pulling at the traces; the reverend instinctively flicked
the reins and the wagon lurched forward, rapidly
gaining momentum as it rattled down the empty street
away from the Crystal Arcade. The reverend heard
another groan and then, to his rear, the noise of something dropping from the wagon.

Any chance of getting away unobserved was now
gone. All he could do was to steer the wagon and try to
get away from the town as quickly as possible. Above the
rattling and swaying of the wagon he became conscious
of shouts coming from the direction of the Crystal
Arcade. The wagon was thundering down the street,
bumping and bouncing and almost throwing the reverend from his seat.

He was approaching the quay and he could see light
glinting on the water ahead of him. He attempted to
turn the wagon as the jetty loomed up but there was no
way he could do it. He hauled hard at the reins in a last
desperate effort to avoid disaster but it was no good.
The spooked horses were not responding and the next
moment the wagon had crashed over the quayside into
the black waters of the Big Muddy. Bent was flung from
his seat as the wagon loomed over him, seeming to float
for a time before slowly leaning sideways and sinking
into the waters. The horses were struggling in the traces
and the reverend swam to them, trying desperately to
set them free.

Lights were moving in the town and people were
approaching the riverbank. Without waiting to see what

might happen next, the reverend began to swim. His clothes were dragging him down and the water felt cold. The current was carrying him downstream and although it was not too far across to the opposite bank, he was finding it hard to make progress towards it. On the quayside people were running about waving flaming brands and shouting. A shot rang out, followed by another. He had no idea how close they were or whether anybody had even seen him. All his efforts were aimed at reaching the opposite bank but his strength was beginning to fade.

He felt himself sinking and with a burst of desperate energy began to beat the water with fierce strokes. He heard more shots and spray spattered into his face. He dipped his head below the surface and continued swimming until his bursting lungs forced him back to the surface. He was disoriented and wasn't sure in which direction he needed to continue. He looked back and saw that the lights on the shore had become more distant. He had travelled a considerable way downstream and he reckoned he was out of reach of any pursuers. Now he needed to gain the shore before his strength finally faded.

Suddenly he became aware of something else in the water beside him. He was confused and couldn't make out what it was. Then he realized that it was a horse. He thought that it must be one of his own horses, which had somehow got free, but as his strength dwindled and he was about to be sucked under by the weight of his garments, he felt an arm reaching down to him. He grasped it. The water was churning with dim shapes that looked like snakes to his confused eyes, then another pair of arms seized him and he felt himself being pulled from the water.

He was on the back of a horse and there was another horse alongside it. He clung on to the rider as the horse swam towards the riverbank, which now was much closer at hand. Both horses were swimming gallantly, their heads raised above the water, then he sensed that their feet had touched bottom. They began to rise out of the water and then they were struggling up the river bank till at last they were clear. The horses came to a halt and he was helped down and laid on the grass. He began to splutter but after a few moments he stopped.

'Guess that just weren't the right sort of sermon,' a voice said.

He opened his eyes and looked up. 'Bannock!' he gasped.

He looked across at the second man. It was Briggs.

'Take it easy. Get your breath back. Here, take this.' Bannock handed him a flask and he took a swallow.

'I don't know as how you approve of whiskey,' the oldster said.

'I approve of it,' the reverend replied.

The whiskey bit but he felt restored. He sat up.

'What in tarnation are you two doin' here?' he said.

Bannock looked back down the river. Flickering lights and an occasional shout indicated the town.

'We're still too close to those varmints for my likin',' he said. 'If you're up to it, Reverend, I figure to put some more distance between us and Cayuse Landing. Then we can build a fire and you can dry off.'

'I'll be OK,' the reverend replied. With an effort he rose to his feet.

'Get up alongside me,' Briggs said.

They mounted up again and set off, moving away from the river. It was late when they eventually stopped. When Bannock and Briggs had a fire going the reverend was able at last to dry out.

'I got a feelin' somethin' like this happened before, only then it was the other way round,' he said. 'I got to thank you boys. I don't reckon I'd have got out of that river without your help.'

When they had eaten the reverend was in a fit state to tell his story. After he had finished Bannock and Briggs explained what had happened to them since leaving him to ride for the Lazy Acre.

'It was just pure luck that we were in town. We'd not long left Jenny in the care of the doc when we heard all the noise and commotion. We didn't expect to find you at the centre of it all. It sure was the dangdest thing to see your wagon in the water!'

The reverend looked pensively at his companions.

'Whichever way we turn,' he said, 'it seems like we come up against Wilder.'

'Yeah, it sure seems that way,' Bannock replied. 'But what do you think he was after with you?'

'I don't know. I just got a feelin' when I saw Sabin that it didn't look good. I guess I was proved right. Like I say, they left some galoot in the back of the wagon to wait for me. I don't know if things were meant to turn out like they did, but I just couldn't afford to take no chances.'

Bannock thought for a moment. 'Wilder's quarrel is with me and Comfort. I figure you just got mixed up in it.'

'If Wilder's lookin' for you,' Briggs said to Bannock, 'he might have figured that the reverend might be able to tell him where to find you.'

'After what happened tonight, Wilder's quarrel with Bannock and Comfort is mine now,' Bent. 'Especially after what you just told me about Jenny.'

'I figured you didn't aim to get mixed up in no violence,' Briggs said. 'It don't seem to square with your preachin'.'

'Yeah. That's what I figured too. Looks like a man sometimes ain't got no choice.'

Bannock did not reply. He was thinking that it was mighty convenient that the reverend had had a gun on him when he got back to the wagon. He certainly seemed to know how to use it.

'Guess I ain't likely to see no more of my wagon,' the reverend mused. 'Or my horses. Even if they got 'em both out of the river.'

'I'm sorry,' Briggs said. 'I suppose all your stuff was in that wagon?'

'It don't matter,' Bent replied. He lapsed into silence.

'It's too late to do anythin' more tonight,' Bannock said. 'I figure we might as well try and catch up on some shut-eye.'

The reverend turned to face him. 'What are you boys plannin' on doin' next?' he said.

'We agreed to meet Comfort at the Black Stirrup. It

123

was kind of a loose arrangement, but I reckon that's what we do.'

'Any objections if I come along?' the reverend asked.

'None at all,' Bannock replied.

'You're forgettin' he ain't got no horse,' Briggs interposed.

'That isn't a problem,' Bannock replied. 'Nobody knows you in Cayuse Landing. You can stop by at the livery stables and pick one up, or even borrow Miss Jenny's.'

'Better get me a rifle,' the reverend said. 'The way things are shapin', I reckon I might be needin' one.'

Spending time at the Lazy Acre had done something to restore Corrina's shattered nerves. Her brother was not badly injured but he needed time and rest for the wound to heal. There was no question of either of them leaving the Lazy Acre in a hurry, so Corrina resolved to make best use of the time. Both Uncle Winslow and Aunt Lucinda were happy to have them stay on, and Aunt Lucinda's ministrations were just what Corrina needed.

As the immediate rawness of the whole episode faded, she began to feel restored. Life took on again its patina of ordinariness and routine. While she felt unwilling to leave the farm, the days passed in a pleasant round of mundane activities; gardening, feeding the hens, helping her aunt with household chores, knitting, reading. She bumped across Harlin occasionally, but it wasn't often and after an initial awkwardness they resumed their familiar roles.

She sometimes thought of the stranger on the boat with the blue eyes, but the recollection faded. She could not now dissociate that encounter from its aftermath, which was reason enough for her to put it away from her.

Just now she was sitting on the veranda, having just come back from a walk with her aunt. It was a fine day. Chickens scuffled in the dust of the yard and the quiet was punctuated by the snuffling of pigs. As she looked out across the fields, she saw a cloud of dust on the track which led up to the farmhouse and after a time a group of riders appeared, among whom she recognized the upright figure of her uncle.

'Aunt Lucinda!' she called.

Her aunt appeared on the doorstep and looked at the approaching group.

'Looks like we've got visitors,' Corrina said.

'Your uncle mentioned something about meeting some folks in town,' Aunt Lucinda replied. 'Looks like he's decided to bring 'em on out to the farm.'

The riders were still some distance away but Aunt Lucinda was able to pick out individuals.

'Well,' she said, 'that's Sam and Joe. No surprise there. I guess they must have finished their work for the day. But ain't that Mr Richards and old Lem Ruddock?'

Noticing Corrina's lack of comprehension, she added: 'Neighbours. They run a couple of farms near by.'

As they got closer, Corrina recognized the two men Aunt Lucinda had referred to as Sam and Joe. They were the same Lazy Acre employees who had been involved in the killing of her molester.

'What are they doing here?' Corrina asked.

Aunt Lucinda shook her head. 'Lords-a-mercy, I don't know nothin' more than I already told you. Winslow don't always let me know just what he's doin'. I ain't sure he always knows himself.'

The riders pulled up in the yard and raised their hats to the two ladies on the veranda before dismounting.

'Good to see you,' Lem Ruddock said. 'You're looking well.'

Aunt Lucinda made a sort of curtsy.

'You're welcome,' she said. 'Although I might have wished my husband had given me some warning.'

Uncle Winslow came up close to his wife and, putting his arm around her, kissed her on the forehead.

'Sorry, Lucinda,' he said. 'We didn't plan on this. Business is takin' a little longer than we reckoned.'

Lucinda turned to the others.

'Well, you'll just have to take us as you find us.'

'These folks will be stayin' overnight. They can use the barn. There should be a few more joinin' us first thing in the morning.'

For the first time Lucinda's face registered concern.

'What's this all about?' she asked.

Winslow hugged her. 'Nothin' you need worry your head about.'

Uncle Winslow introduced Corrina to the two farmers, whom she had not met before. Harlin appeared to deal with the horses. As they went inside, Corrina couldn't help but notice that, for a meeting of farmers, they all appeared to be well armed. She had a curious intimation that their presence was somehow due to her and felt a flickering suggestion of the feeling she thought she'd got over: that unsettling sensation of suddenly peering into an abyss. Just at that moment the door to the bedroom where Daniel had been recuperating flew open and Daniel appeared.

'What are you doing out of bed?' Aunt Lucinda said.

Daniel advanced into the room. 'I'm all right, Aunty,' he said. 'I shoulda been up and about days ago.'

He moved across the floor to where his uncle was standing. 'I saw you comin' and I reckon I can guess what's goin' on,' he said. 'Well, I'm comin' right along with you.'

His uncle looked at him closely. For a moment he seemed to consider the boy's words then he nodded.

'You got as big a stake in this as any of the rest of us,' he said. 'That varmint who dry-gulched you was one of Wilder's boys. We all got reason to want him dealt with. If you feel you're fit to ride with us, I ain't gonna say no.'

It was very late when Comfort and Annie turned in for the night and daylight had spread across the sky before they began to stir. Neither of them seemed keen to get moving, and they took their time over breakfast.

'I sure am glad that you found Jenny safe and well,' Annie said. 'If I'd taken the main trail out of Cayuse Landing I might have caught up with her myself.'

'You assumed she'd been taken by Wilder?'

'What else was I to think after what happened last time?'

127

'Sure. I guess it made sense to take the trail towards the Black Stirrup.'

'I would have rode right on in but it got late and I wanted time to think. I guess it was just as well.'

They finished breakfast. Annie poured coffee for them both.

'You say you were headin' for the Lazy Acre?' Annie said.

'Yeah.'

'That time, you know, when you were sick and I helped to look after you . . .'

'You didn't just help. If it hadn't have been for you, I would never have pulled through.'

'That's as maybe. I was goin' to say that you told me then about Laidler. Seems kinda strange, don't it, that after all this time, you should be led right here. I know Winslow Clayburne. It seems even stranger that he should be the very person you've been lookin' for. I know him. Not well, but a little. Are you sure he's the same man?'

'Pretty sure. And so is Briggs. He reckons that Clayburne knows about him too.'

They fell silent until Annie spoke again.

'So what are you gonna do now?' she said. 'Are you gonna ride on to the Lazy Acre?'

Comfort looked at her and it seemed to him there was more to that question than her words implied. He felt a strange inertia. It was good to be sitting beside her. Suddenly he felt he didn't want to leave her. It seemed to him almost not to matter what he did next as long as she was with him. He was casting about in his

128

mind for an answer when all thoughts were driven away by a sound which came to his ears and which he identified at once, faint though it was. It was the sound of galloping horses. Annie heard it too and a look of alarm spread across her features.

'Could it be your friends Bannock and Briggs?' she asked.

He shook his head. 'Too many of 'em,' he said. 'Maybe Wilder realizes we're here. Whoever it is, we'd best find shelter.'

Without wasting a moment's time he jumped up and kicked out the fire, pouring the rest of the coffee on to the embers. Then they gathered up their things and mounted their horses. Comfort looked about him. Away to their right the land rose towards some low hills.

'We'll head that way,' he said. 'There's a better chance of finding cover.'

Applying their spurs, they rode hard in the direction Comfort had indicated. The breeze blew the sound of horses to their ears but, looking back, Comfort could see no sign of riders yet. One thing struck him. The riders were coming from the direction in which he had been riding with Bannock and Briggs when they found Jenny. It might not mean anything, but it was not the direction of the Black Stirrup.

They continued riding till they were among the low-lying hills. Away off the trail some rocky outcrops stood up out of the surrounding terrain.

'Over that way!' Comfort shouted.

They turned off the trail they had been following and continued to ride hard till they found themselves approaching the rocks, when they drew rein.

'We'll get down here and hide the horses behind those boulders,' Comfort said.

Quickly, they led the horses into the shelter of the rocks and then, taking their rifles, took position themselves behind a screen of rocks and scrub. Comfort regarded Annie's rifle.

'You know how to fire that thing?' he said.

She smiled. 'Yes, of course I do.' She drew aside her coat enough for him to see the handle of the Smith & Wesson in her belt. 'I know how to fire this too,' she said.

Comfort nodded. 'There shouldn't be any need to use them,' he said, 'but it don't pay to take no chances.'

She closed her jacket and as she moved to adjust her position she slipped and bumped against Comfort. He put out a hand to steady her and looked down at the same moment that she looked up at him. Without realizing what he was doing, he put his hand behind her head and, drawing his face to hers, kissed her on the lips.

'I was hopin' you'd do that,' she said.

He kissed her again, then glanced over her head along the trail they had ridden.

'Do you see anything?' she said.

A cloud of dust was moving across the landscape, coming in their direction. They both sat up and observed its passage. Comfort put his field glasses to his eyes. He could discern about a dozen riders.

'Which way is the Black Stirrup?' Comfort said.

Annie pointed along the trail they had turned off.

130

'It could be a bunch of Wilder's boys headed back from town,' Annie said.

'If it is, there's an awful lot of 'em and they seem to be comin' from the wrong direction, unless they took the long way round.'

They continued to watch. The riders were making rapid progress and soon they were approaching the spot where Comfort and Annie had made camp. Comfort was expecting them to ride on but instead they drew to a halt. He looked closely though the field glasses.

'What's happening?' Annie breathed.

Two of the riders seemed to be consulting one another. Comfort handed the glasses to Annie.

'Do you recognize any of 'em?' he asked.

She took the glasses and took a long look through them.

'I don't recognize any of them as Wilder's boys,' she said, 'but I got a feeling I know the one who's doing most of the talking.'

'Yeah? Who is it?'

She put the glasses down, then raised them again to take another look.

'I don't know him that well and I might be mistaken, but I reckon that could be Clayburne!'

'Clayburne? The owner of the Lazy Acre? Here, let me take another look.'

Comfort almost snatched the glasses from her grip. He clapped them to his eyes.

'Which one?' he said.

'The older one. The man with the white hair and beard.'

131

Comfort concentrated his attention on the man. There was something about him which looked vaguely familiar, but he couldn't be certain that he recognized him.

'So that's Clayburne. I wonder what he's doin' out here?'

As he looked the two men ceased talking and the next moment the whole bunch of riders began to move towards where he and Annie lay concealed.

'Hell!' Comfort said. 'They must have seen our sign. They're comin' this way.'

He looked about him, considering whether the best option might be to run for it. Then he considered: what had they to fear from Clayburne? Clayburne might have got wise to Briggs, but he had no way of knowing who Comfort was, much less what he was doing here. He decided on a plan.

'Before they get here,' he said, 'I'll step out of cover.'

'No!' she said.

'Listen. I'll just make out I'm passin' through. There's no reason why there should be trouble.'

'They'll know there are two horses.'

'I can make out one is a packhorse. You just stay out of sight. They'll probably just head right on.'

'They took the bother of turning off to come up here,' Annie replied.

'Do like I say. Go on back further into the rocks. Leave it to me.'

Reluctantly, Annie did as Comfort wanted. When he was satisfied that she was well out of sight, Comfort moved forward and sat down in the open with his back against a rock. He laid his rifle down where he could quickly reach it if he needed to, then dug into his shirt for his packet of Bull Durham. He built himself a smoke and sat back to wait as the riders drew closer. Once he looked closely through his field glasses at the figure of Clayburne; the years had wrought a considerable change in him, yet he thought he could, after all, discern the old features beneath the changes. He wondered for a moment what the years had done to himself. Would Clayburne recognize him? The situation was different. Clayburne – Laidler – had been in charge of the camp. He had been one prisoner among thousands. It was unlikely Clayburne would ever have remembered him.

CHAPTER SEVEN

The riders were getting quite close now. Comfort's eyes scanned the group, looking for any clue to their make-up or their purposes. A couple of them looked tough, but in the main they looked pretty ordinary; they might have been townsfolk or farmers or ordinary cowpokes. Certainly Clayburne appeared to be their leader. The one he had been talking to was a much younger man. Comfort had a vague feeling that he had seen him somewhere before but he couldn't think where. It had been quite recently.

Suddenly, with a shock, he thought he recognized him. It was the young man he had met on the boat: Corrina's brother. As they approached he flicked aside the stub of his cigarette and stood up. As he did so there was a loud crash which went echoing and rever-berating among the rocks and the boulder against which he had been sitting splintered as shards of stone flew into the air.

Instantly Comfort reached for his rifle as a second shot rang out and a bullet plucked at the sleeve of his coat. From among the rocks behind him an answering shot bellowed and one of the riders fell from his horse. With a leap Comfort was behind the rock as shots began to fly all about him. Once within shelter, he levelled his rifle and opened fire. The noise was deafening as a hail of bullets tore into the rocks. It continued for a few minutes, then there was a sudden silence till a voice cut through it like a thunderclap.

'You ain't gettin' away. You're gonna die, you and all of Wilder's stinkin' coyotes.'

The words were followed by a fresh burst of gunfire which went echoing around the rocks. Comfort peered round the boulder. Clayburne and his men had dismounted and taken cover. He could see their horses further down the trail but he could see nothing of their riders. He quickly estimated their relative positions and came to the conclusion that it didn't look good. He could probably hold them off for a fair while, but he was outgunned. Sooner or later they would get him.

The main immediate danger, as he saw it, was that some of them might try to outflank him. He had a pretty good view in front but there were bushes on both sides which would provide cover to anyone trying to get behind him. And he had Annie to think about. He realized that the shot which had lifted one of Clayburne's men out of the saddle, and which had probably saved him, had come from Annie. She was right about being able to handle a rifle.

He wanted to call to her but he didn't want to give away the fact that he was not alone. He hoped she would have enough sense not to let her position be known. But that one shot had probably been enough to give her away. Clayburne had probably worked that out by now.

Taking advantage of another slight lull in the shooting, he called out in reply to Clayburne, hoping that he might be able to deflect Clayburne's anger.

'I don't know anyone called Wilder! Whoever he is, I ain't got nothin' to do with him!'

The response was a fresh burst of gunfire and he realized the futility of trying to deter his attackers. They had convinced themselves that he was one of Wilder's men and, whatever reason they had for riding against Wilder, they didn't intend to spare him. He thought of his days in the prison camp and the Laidler he had known. Maybe the man hadn't changed so much after all. The gunfire quieted and Clayburne's voice called out again.

'We've had enough of you scum. You made a big mistake when you shot my brother's boy.'

'I don't know nothin' about your brother's boy!' Comfort replied.

'You or Wilder; it don't make no difference. As far as I'm concerned, it don't matter just who pulled that trigger! You're all guilty!'

Comfort raised his head a fraction above the rock, thinking he might get a glimpse of Clayburne. He realized his mistake as a bullet thudded into the rock a few inches from his skull. He pulled back and instead began to inch backwards, thinking to get to Annie.

As he did so a shot rang out somewhere above him, answered immediately by another from his rear. He heard a groan and glanced up to see a puff of smoke ascending from the face of the rocky outcrop above him. He realized at once that Annie had replied to the first shot, and he also realized that the thing he had feared was coming to pass. At least one of their attackers had managed to gain a position where he could fire down on him.

Doubled over, he made his way back to where Annie had taken shelter, taking care to apprise her of the fact it was him and not one of Clayburne's men.

'Annie, are you OK?' he breathed.

'Sure. I told you I could handle a gun.'

He grinned briefly. 'The question is, what do we do next?' he said. 'We can hold out for a time but there's too many of 'em.'

'I heard Clayburne calling out,' she replied. 'Is there no way we can make him see that we haven't anything to do with Wilder?'

'I tried but it's no good. Clayburne's convinced himself I'm one of Wilder's men.'

'We're on Wilder's land,' Annie replied.

'I'd better be gettin' back in position,' Comfort said. 'You make sure to keep out of sight. I'll think of somethin'.'

He made his way back. Bullets were flying overhead but Clayburne seemed to have settled on a policy of patience. At least a couple of his men had been hit and it seemed he was prepared to take a little time to gain his quarry.

Comfort waited for a time, holding his fire, trying to decide what to do next. He could stay where he was

137

GUNS OF WRATH

with relative safety, but it seemed to him that if he and
Annie were to have any chance, albeit a slim one, of
getting out of the situation alive, he needed to do something more positive.

Keeping low, he began to inch along sideways in an
attempt to gain a higher vantage point and a different
angle from which he might be able to do more damage.
He pushed through a patch of shrub and scrambled
over some more rocks which were tumbled together till
he reached a high point from which he was better able
to survey the scene, but he was disappointed.
Clayburne's men had hidden themselves well.

A shot pinged off one of the rocks near by and he
ducked. Someone had seen him. The position was
getting serious. From where he was positioned he could
not see Annie but occasional explosions from that
direction told him she was still returning fire. He had
an idea. Maybe he could get to their horses and loose
them. He looked over but the horses were too far away
and to reach them he would have to cross a patch of
open ground.

He was about to turn his head away when he saw a
cloud of dust similar to the one Clayburne's men had
made but smaller. It could only be more riders heading
in their direction. Who could it be? They were coming
from the general direction of the Black Stirrup and his
first thoughts were that it must be some of Wilder's
boys. Wilder must have realized that something was
happening on a remote stretch of his property and he
was coming to investigate.

He remembered his field glasses and put them to his

eyes. There were only three riders. Wouldn't Wilder have come with a bigger force? He looked again and then his heart gave a thump. Two of the riders were Bannock and Briggs. He stared hard trying to see who the third man was, then he realized it was the reverend. What was he doing with Bannock and Briggs?

It didn't matter. The arrival of his friends might be enough to save him and Annie. They would still be considerably outnumbered, but it gave them a fighting chance. With a last glance towards the approaching trio, he began to climb down in order to reach Annie and apprise her of the changing situation.

As he did so he became aware that the firing from Clayburne's men had dwindled. Someone began to shout and he realized that Clayburne had seen the approach of the riders. For a few moments more the quiet continued and then there was a fresh eruption of firing, but this time it was not aimed at him. He scrambled over the remaining rocks and reached Annie.

'What's happening?' she said.

'Bannock's showed up. Remember I told you about Briggs and the reverend? They're both with him.'

'The reverend? You mean the Reverend Bent?' Annie looked confused.

'I don't know how come he's ridin' with them either, but it gives us a chance,' Comfort snapped.

His brow creased in thought. 'You stay here,' he said. 'I'll go back and see what I can do from this side. I guess Bannock and the others will have taken cover. Between us, we might be able to pin Clayburne down.'

He started to move away but Annie caught his arm.

'I'm comin' with you,' she said. 'We're gonna need all the firepower we can muster.'

For a second he hesitated but Annie was already on her feet and he saw there was no point in trying to dissuade her.

'Keep your head down and be careful,' he said.

Together, they made their way back to where Comfort had taken his original station. A couple of bullets flew harmlessly among the rocks but most of the shooting was now taking place in front of them. Positioning themselves behind the rocks, they opened fire, aiming at the flashes of flame and smoke which issued from the rocks and bushes behind which Clayburne and his men had taken cover.

They had positioned themselves well. Comfort could still see nothing of them and they had spread out so they had a comprehensive view of what was happening around them. He could see nothing of his friends and he tried calling out to them but his words were lost in the rattle of gunfire. Bannock must have guessed, however, who it was under attack. He was no fool. He could put two and together. Except, in this case, he probably assumed it was Wilder doing the attacking.

Comfort glanced at Annie. She sure was game. She had run out of ammunition for the rifle and was now using the Smith & Wesson. It didn't matter that her fire was probably ineffective; her hand was steady and she showed no sign of fear. The sound of firing swelled in a crescendo and then as quickly diminished. Comfort and Annie exchanged glances. Cautiously, Comfort looked over the top of the boulder he was hiding behind. Gunsmoke and the smell of gunpowder drifted on the air but a strange silence had descended. Then Comfort became aware of noises; the sound of voices, the jingling of harness and then the thud of horses' hoofs.

'Don't move,' he said to Annie. 'I'll be back in a moment.'

He quickly made his way back to the more elevated spot where he had first seen Bannock and the others coming. Clayburne and his men had taken to their horses and were riding hard away from the outcrop in the direction of the Black Stirrup. Quickly, he swung down to rejoin Annie.

'Clayburne's taken off,' he said.

Gingerly, he raised himself above the level of the sheltering rock.

'Be careful!' Annie hissed.

He stepped over the intervening rocks and into the clear. His senses were stretched and he was alert to the slightest indication of movement, but nothing stirred. Away off to his left he could see dust where Clayburne's men were heading off. The sudden silence was uncanny. Raising his voice, he called out:

'Bannock! Are you there?'

His words sounded especially loud and he felt almost as if he were committing some kind of sacrilege. Then, to his relief, there came an answering call:

'Comfort? Are you OK?'

'Yeah! I think it's safe to come out of cover!'

He heard a footfall behind him and turned to see Annie approaching. They stood together while in front

141

of them the bushes parted and Bannock and Briggs stepped out, followed after a moment by the reverend.

'You old son of a gun!' Bannock exclaimed.

'Hell, I sure am glad to see you.'

They strode forward and seized one another by the hand. When they had exchanged greetings Bannock turned to Comfort.

'What was the meaning of all that?' he said. 'And why did Wilder decide to run?'

'That wasn't Wilder,' Comfort said. 'That was Clayburne. And I figure he rode off to do what he came out here to do in the first place.'

Bannock whistled. 'Clayburne? What happened? Did you confront him?'

'Nope. I had nothin' to do with it. Me and Annie were just a kind of sideshow. I reckon his target is Wilder. And the fact that he's abandoned this little scrap means he's carryin' right on to the Black Stirrup.'

'I've heard rumours.' Annie said. 'This has been simmering up for a long time. Wilder has been pushing the farmers around for too long. He's been making threats, trying to buy them out for less than their farms are worth. There may be something else behind it, but it was probably coming one day.'

'Clayburne shouted somethin' about his brother's boy gettin' shot.'

'That would probably be enough to tip him over,' Briggs said. 'Despite appearances, it seems he ain't the type to let things go. Remember he somehow got word about me askin' about him and sent his boys after me to Greenoak.'

142

Comfort was about to say something in reply when suddenly a shot rang out. Annie gave a scream and reeled backwards. Comfort spun round. A figure was just disappearing behind a rock. In a flash Comfort's gun was in his hand and spitting lead. The shot crashed into the rock, missing its target by inches. The man disappeared but Comfort was running fast in pursuit. Without pausing, he rounded the rock. A little way ahead of him the man was running fast. Comfort paused for a second, then ran on as the man disappeared from sight into some thick scrub. Comfort rushed on but before he reached the spot where the man had gone his foot slipped and he went crashing to the ground. In an instant he was back on his feet. He plunged into the undergrowth but he could not see where the man had gone.

He had begun to move forward when he heard the sound of a horse near by, and as he emerged into a glade he saw the man riding off. The man turned and fired a shot which crashed into the bushes next to where Comfort was standing. He carried on running, although he knew it was no use. Without a horse he could never catch the man. Still he kept going, when to his surprise a group of three other riders appeared ahead of him, riding out of cover to join the man who had shot at Annie. They were riding hard away from him.

He dropped down on one knee and loosed off a shot with his revolver, but they were already out of range. Without delaying further Comfort ran back to where he had left the others. Annie lay on the ground with

Bannock and the reverend bending over her.

'Annie!' Comfort cried.

Her eyes were closed but they flickered open at his arrival.

'Is she hurt bad?'

'I don't know,' Bannock said.

Annie's mouth opened. 'Will,' she muttered weakly.

Comfort knelt down beside her.

'Will, I'm so glad you came back to Cayuse Landing.'

Her eyes closed and Comfort felt a wave of anguish seize him. Then her eyes opened once again and she smiled at him.

'Give me your bandanna,' the reverend said.

Briggs and Bannock both undid their neckties. The reverend knelt down, tied them together and began to fasten them tightly round her upper leg.

'The bullet's gone through her thigh,' he said to Comfort. 'It's a clean wound. If we can just stop the bleeding she'll probably be all right.'

Annie seemed to gather her strength and even attempted to sit up.

'Take it easy,' the reverend said.

'Those goddamned varmints,' Comfort muttered. 'I don't care which one it is. Wilder or Clayburne, they're as bad as each other. They're both responsible for this.'

Annie looked up at him and her mouth opened as if she was about to speak again.

'What is it?' Comfort said.

Comfort had a feeling that her reluctance to speak was not on account of her injury.

'Do you want to tell me somethin'?' he said. 'You're

not hurt anywhere else?'

She shook her head gently before speaking.

'The man who shot me,' she said. 'I saw him just before he fired. It wasn't one of Clayburne's men. It was Carl Sabin.'

'Sabin? The same man beat you up and took Jenny?'

She nodded again. Comfort leaped to his feet.

'What are you doin', Comfort?' Bannock shouted.

'I'm goin' after Sabin and the rest of the varmints.'

Bannock and Briggs exchanged glances.

'You can't go up against them alone,' Bannock shouted.

Comfort strode on, looking for his horse.

'What can one man do against all of Wilder's gunnies?' Briggs called.

Bannock turned to the reverend.

'You stay here and keep an eye on Miss Annie,' he said.

The reverend scrutinized him.

'What are you aimin' to do?' he said.

Again Bannock and Briggs looked at one another. Briggs nodded imperceptibly.

'Hold it, Comfort!' Bannock shouted. 'Just give us time to get our horses. We're comin' with you.'

Before they got close to the Black Stirrup, they could hear the sounds of shooting.

'Give Clayburne his due,' Briggs said. 'He ain't afraid to go straight to the heart of the matter.'

'I wonder how many of the others feel the same way?' Bannock replied. 'If some of those boys are regular

145

farmers, they may not like it when things hot up.'

'Wilder must have driven them hard. Sooner or later the worm turns.'

Comfort ignored their comments. His jaw was set and his blue eyes flashed their intensity. Only when they had their first glimpse of the ranch house did they draw rein.

'What now?' Bannock said.

They sat their horses and surveyed the scene. The ranch house was built on rising ground, overlooked at the back by a gently sloping wooded hill. It was clear that Clayburne had Wilder pinned down in the ranch house. Puffs of smoke rose from the trees and stabs of flame appeared at the ranch house windows.

'I don't imagine Wilder would have expected this,' Bannock said.

'Yeah. Guess they caught him by surprise.'

Bannock laughed. 'Well, I guess the best thing we can do is just let 'em fight it out.'

Comfort could see the sense of the oldster's comment, but he was growing restless. Things had turned out a lot different from what he had anticipated, but he was dissatisfied. Wilder and Clayburne might destroy each other and he could sit back and watch them do it, but he had a personal interest in the affair. It was not Clayburne who occupied his mind now, but Wilder.

He thought about the things that had happened since his arrival at Cayuse Landing. From the moment he had set foot in the Crystal Arcade his life had been set at nought by Wilder and his boys. Without

Bannock's help, he would have been gunned down that first day. He remembered what had happened to the pair of them since; how Wilder's gunnies had waited for them at Bannock's shack, how they burned it down. He thought about Jenny. More than that, he thought about how Wilder had treated Annie.

Now Annie had been shot, and it seemed by Wilder's man: Sabin. It was a fair guess that Sabin and the three other riders with him had been on their way back from Cayuse Landing. Watching what was happening at Wilder's ranch, it was as if everything had narrowed down for him to those two names. Wilder and Sabin.

'I'm ridin' on down,' he said.

Bannock and Briggs looked at each other.

'You can't do that,' Briggs said. 'It would be suicide.'

'I'll take my chances,' Comfort said.

Bannock's horse reared as the sound of gunfire momentarily grew louder.

'What are you tryin' to prove?' Bannock said after bringing it back under control. 'Why not wait here and see what happens?'

'I've waited long enough,' Comfort replied.

Without waiting for an answer, he touched his spurs to the horse's flanks.

'He's got to be crazy,' Bannock said.

Comfort rode at a steady pace towards the ranch house, directing his course towards the smoke-filled yard. As he rode, his eyes scanned the scene. Most of Clayburne's men had taken cover in the trees on the hillside, but a few seemed to have worked their way round to some corrals at the back, from where they were attempting to storm the rear of the ranch house. In the corrals horses were stamping and tossing. He wondered how long it would take before somebody on either side spotted him.

A kind of calm recklessness had taken possession of him. It was as if all the years of pain and bitterness had come to a head and formed an abscess which needed to be punctured. He wasn't thinking. He had no plan of action, no firm idea of what he would do when he got within range of both side's guns. It was as if something outside himself had taken over, or some deeper part of himself that didn't require conscious thought.

The din of the guns was getting louder the nearer he got to the ranch house. His horse's head was up and its ears were pricked but it seemed to have taken on something of its rider's resoluteness and it did not falter.

He was getting close when a plume of smoke suddenly arose from the back of the ranch house and flames began pouring through the roof. Within moments a cloud of billowing smoke obscured the yard, mingling with gunsmoke. Comfort spurred his horse and began to gallop fast. The scene in front of him was one of confusion. Shooting had dwindled and above the sporadic bark of guns he could hear voices calling frantically.

A couple of figures had emerged from hiding and were running towards the barn. The door of the ranch house flew open and some men emerged, running hard for cover. A few horses seemed to have escaped from the corral and were running and plunging through the yard. Into this mêlée Comfort stormed.

Out of the smoke a figure loomed up but Comfort did not stop. The horse hit the man full on and he went hurtling to the ground. As the horse veered, Comfort slid from the saddle and ran towards the ranch house door. Smoke was pouring from inside but he did not stop.

Once inside, he was met by a wall of heat. Flames were licking through an open door beyond which the fire raged. The crackle of the flames was loud but not loud enough to drown a frenzied cry for help. Pulling up his bandanna for protection, Comfort crashed through the door. He could see nothing at first because of the smoke and dancing flames but after a moment he saw a figure lying on the floor. Between him and the man stretched a wall of fire but he didn't hesitate. He leapt through the flames with one bound, bent down and, hauling the man upright, hoisted him over his shoulder.

He turned to retrace his steps but the fire was raging with renewed fury and there was no way back. Staggering under the weight of his burden, he made for the back of the room where a blown-out window offered the only possible way of escape. He turned his back to the scorched window frame and unceremoniously dumped the man through it. He was wilting and it took all his remaining willpower to climb out of the window himself. He landed next to the man he had rescued and, coughing and spluttering, began to drag him away from the tortured building.

His lungs were bursting and he had little strength left to attempt to lift the man. He had succeeded in

149

getting him halfway to the corral when the ranch house walls gave way and the rear of the building collapsed in a shower of sparks. He had no time to dwell on what was happening because, with a thunder of hoofs, the remaining horses broke loose from the corral and began to gallop wildly in all directions.

A fresh burst of fire came from the front of the building and a group of men emerged from a corner of the building behind him. A couple of shots rang out and bullets thudded into the earth near by. He drew his revolver and swivelled, taking an instant to steady himself before returning fire. The men had spread out and they had him covered. He dropped to the ground, rolling away as more bullets tore up dust. The situation was bad but then he became aware that the men had turned away and were not firing at him, but at someone behind them.

Taking advantage of the moment, he leaped to his feet and, seizing the inert form of the man he had rescued from the fire, drew him into the relative safety of some bushes alongside the corral. Then he ducked back to face his attackers, but when he looked two of them lay stretched on the ground and the others were running hell for leather for the barn. Round the corner of the burning building two figures emerged, their guns smoking. Comfort raised his gun, about to fire, when he saw that the two men were Bannock and Briggs.

'Go easy with that shooter!' Bannock yelled.

They ran to join him.

'What the—' Comfort began when the oldster broke in:

150

'You might be mad, Comfort, but you didn't think we'd let you do it on your own?'

'What's happening?' Comfort said.

'Looks like Clayburne's won the day. Wilder's men cut and run once the fire took hold.'

Bannock looked more closely at Comfort. 'You're singed,' he said.

Comfort became aware that he had suffered burns in the fire. The skin of his hands was blistered and his clothes had suffered badly. He remembered the man he had rescued.

'Come here,' he said.

Bannock and Briggs followed him to where he had laid the man down.

'I don't know how bad he is,' Comfort said.

Bannock bent down, took one glance, then looked up at Comfort.

'Hell, you realize who this is? It's only Clayburne himself!'

Comfort had been in no position to observe anything about the man he had saved from the fire. Even if he had, it was unlikely he would have recognized him from the glimpse he had had through his field glasses, especially in his present condition. Clayburne's face was burnt, blackened and blistered.

Before Comfort could grasp the situation or react, they heard the clatter of feet and two men appeared from the bushes at the side of the corral. Bannock and Briggs had them covered. Looking up, Comfort thought he recognized the younger of them.

'Have you seen Clayburne?' one of them asked.

Bannock indicated the prostrate figure of Clayburne with his gun. The young man sprang to his side.

'He's alive,' he said. 'Here, help me carry him to the barn.'

'You got this man to thank for that,' Briggs said.

The young man looked at Comfort and Comfort realized who he was.

'You're Corrina Stead's brother,' he said.

The youngster's face expressed surprise. 'Where have I seen you before?'

'The paddle steamer,' Comfort said. 'Hope you managed those cases.'

Daniel did not wait for further elucidation. Instead, he lifted up his uncle and, with some assistance from Briggs, carried him into the barn. As they did so, there came another tremendous crash as the rest of the ranch house collapsed. The last of the shooting had died away. As they tended to Clayburne, a man entered the barn. Daniel looked up at his arrival.

'Well, he said, 'have you found any trace of Wilder?'

The man was breathless and paused to recover before replying.

'Looks like he got away. Him and his henchman Sabin.'

Daniel looked angry. 'What do you mean, he got away?'

'I asked around. Lem Ruddock said he thought he saw them both ridin' off just about the time the ranch took fire.'

Daniel made to move but then stopped and looked at the burned body of Clayburne.

'It's OK,' Comfort said. 'Leave those two to me.'

Daniel hesitated then nodded.

'Did he see which way they went?' Comfort asked the newcomer.

'Towards town.'

'You mean Cayuse Landing?'

'Yeah.'

Comfort got as far as the entrance to the barn when Bannock stopped him.

'You ain't ridin' off alone again?' he said.

Comfort took the oldster's shoulder.

'I appreciate it,' he said. 'I appreciate how you and Briggs helped me out of a tough corner again. I guess I was kinda hasty. But this time I figure it's my fight.'

The oldster looked unconvinced.

'Just get back to the reverend and make sure Annie's all right.' Comfort released his hold and glanced towards Briggs. 'You understand?' he said.

Briggs nodded. Comfort walked out of the barn into the heat from the fire.

'See you at Annie's place in Cayuse Landing,' he called over his shoulder.

It didn't take him long to find his horse. Thankfully, it had emerged unscathed from all the mayhem. He climbed into leather and rode away. When he reached the bottom of the slope leading to the Black Stirrup he stopped to look back. Flames still rose into the air but they were dying down. Nothing much remained of the ranch house but a blackened mass of twisted timber. A few people were gathered in the yard in front. Bodies of men and horses lay around and some of the horses that had broken loose from the corral still wandered about. Then he pulled on the reins and set his course for Cayuse Landing.

It was only when he was out of sight and sound of the Black Stirrup and riding steadily that the implications of what he had done began to dawn on him. He had saved Laidler from the fire. Far from carrying out his revenge, he had rescued his enemy, saved him from a horrible death. He had set out to do one thing and he had done the precise opposite. How could it have happened?

He fell to wondering whether it would have made any difference if he had known who the man was in that blazing room; he couldn't arrive at a definite answer. The facts remained. Where did that put him now? Maybe Laidler, or Clayburne as he was now known, wouldn't pull through. Either way, it made no difference. The deed was done. Now he had other matters to attend to.

The miles passed but he scarcely noticed. He had not even taken account of the direction he was travelling but late in the afternoon he came on the old weathered sign pointing towards Cayuse Landing. So far he hadn't considered what he would do when he got there, but now he needed to have his wits about him. Wilder had fled the scene of the battle, together with Sabin. Why had he done so? It could only have been because he realized he was losing that particular fight, but he would surely not give up so easily.

Not all of his men would have been involved in the affair. He was too powerful to be defeated so easily. He would probably gather more of his men and regroup. That would probably mean the end for the farmers he was attempting to buy out. Did they realize the situation? Once Wilder was back in action, he wouldn't be likely to show any mercy. He could rebuild the Black Stirrup, but he would never forgive its destruction. There was only one way Wilder would be finally defeated, and that would be when he was put permanently out of the picture.

Comfort began to have a sense of how much depended on him. The future of the whole town rested on his shoulders. More than that: Wilder controlled most of the river traffic and his influence extended to the region beyond. It seemed he was aiming to extend his influence by running out the farmers. Unconsciously Comfort shrugged. He simply remembered Annie and the way Wilder had treated her. None of the rest of it was his problem.

He was coming up to the outskirts of town. It was getting quite late in the afternoon but there was still a considerable number of townsfolk about. Something about him must have attracted their attention because several people stopped in their tracks to watch him as he rode by. A man loading up a wagon outside the general store paused in the act of raising a sack to his shoulder. The blacksmith, in the process of beating out a sheet of iron, laid down his hammer and moved to the door of his forge. Comfort looked straight ahead but his gaze swept the street.

A number of horses were tied to the hitch rack outside the Crystal Arcade. Coming abreast of it, he remained in the saddle for a few more moments before sliding from the leather. He tied his horse to the rail and bent over to look at the other horses. Two of them carried the Black Stirrup brand and they bore the sweat and dust of the trail. They had been ridden very recently. He stood back to take one last glance up and down the street, then, stepping up to the boardwalk, he brushed through the batwing doors.

Through a haze of smoke he saw two men standing at the bar and something told him they were the two he was after. He strode slowly through the room. Heads turned and the background noise dropped. A tense stillness descended and the bartender paused as he dried a glass. The two men at the bar sensed that something was happening and glanced in the long mirror.

'Wilder!' Comfort said. One of the men slowly moved. 'I hear you been lookin' for me. Well here I am.'

Wilder turned round so that his back was to the bar. He looked Comfort up and down through flat, cruel eyes.

'And who are you?' he hissed.

'It don't matter. Just call me a friend of Beaver Bannock.'

A flicker of understanding passed across Wilder's face.

'You're makin' a big mistake,' he said.

The other man turned. Even though he hadn't met him, Comfort would have recognized him from Annie's description.

'You ain't facin' a woman this time, Sabin,' Comfort said.

Sabin's lip twisted in a snarl and his eyes flickered. Reflected in the mirror behind him, Comfort could see one of the seated customers slowly reaching beneath the table.

Without hesitation he turned and as the man's gun appeared in his hand he fired twice. The man slumped and his chair went crashing to the floor. Comfort spun back and as Sabin's finger squeezed the trigger of his gun he fired again. Sabin staggered back, blood pouring from his chest; his gun exploded but Comfort had leaned sideways and the bullet flew past his shoulder. He fired again and Sabin went down, falling heavily against the bar. Comfort dropped to one knee but as he did so felt the heavy impact of a bullet and a searing pain in his arm. His gun fell from his hand as he looked up into the leering face of Wilder.

'Like I said, you made a big mistake,' Wilder sneered.

Wilder lifted his gun. Comfort flung himself forward in a desperate bid to grapple with his opponent but Wilder was too quick and stepped aside. With a contemptuous smirk across his features he raised his gun but before his finger closed on the trigger a shot rang out and he staggered back. Comfort glanced in the direction of the stairs; standing on the middle landing he saw the figure of Jenny. In her hand was a smoking derringer. As he watched she dropped the weapon and sank to the stairs, sobbing.

He turned back to his would-be killer. Wilder's eyes

were wide in astonishment. He opened his mouth as though to speak as blood oozed from a hole in his forehead. He looked at Comfort as though to ask a question, then fell forward at Comfort's feet.

After the boom of gunfire an eerie silence filled the room. Comfort bent down to examine the bodies of Wilder and Sabin. Both were dead. The pain in his upper arm began to make itself felt but he knew he wasn't badly hurt. He also knew how lucky he was. Even though she was only a matter of a few feet away from Wilder, the chances were slim that Jenny's bullet would have proved fatal. He moved to the staircase and, climbing the few stairs to the landing, raised Jenny to her feet.

'It's all right,' he said, trying to soothe her.

'I came back to get my things,' she said inconsequentially.

Below them, the Crystal Arcade was stirring back into life. Together, they descended the stairs and walked towards the door. Nobody made any attempt to stop them. As they were about to step through the batwings, Comfort turned back.

'You got a chance to make this a decent town,' he said.

A few people began to murmur and someone gave a cheer. Comfort and Jenny pushed through the batwings into the clear light of day.

'You stayin'at the doc's place?' Comfort asked.

Jenny nodded.

'Guess you'd better take me there,' Comfort said.

*

A few days had passed. Both Annie and Comfort were responding well to treatment. Annie was getting around with the help of a stick and Comfort's right arm was in a sling. They were both sitting on the veranda of Annie's house together with Bannock, Briggs and the reverend when Jenny put her head round the door.

'There's some people to see you,' she said.

Annie looked up.

'To see me?'

'They didn't say. More for Mr Comfort, I think.'

Comfort got to his feet and walked through the house. Sitting outside in a carriage were two people he had not expected to see. One was Daniel Stead and the other was his sister Corrina. Something stirred in Comfort's chest at the sight of her and she blushed at his approach. Then she seemed to notice his sling for the first time and concern spread across her features.

'You're hurt!' she said.

'It's nothin' serious,' Comfort said.

Their eyes met, then she looked away.

'We heard somethin' about what happened between you and Wilder,' Daniel said. 'I think the whole town is in your debt. You know the marshal has resigned and the town council is meeting to appoint a new one?'

'Yeah? Well, that's a good sign.'

There was an awkward pause.

'We were passing by,' Daniel said. 'We had some business in town and now we're just on our way back to Willow.'

'You didn't think of taking a boat this time?' Comfort said, making an effort to keep things light.

'We just wanted to thank you for everything, and especially for what you did for our uncle.' Corrina looked at him again. 'It was very brave of you,' she added.

Comfort didn't know what to say. He felt very uncomfortable.

'How is your uncle?' he said.

'His burns are quite bad but he'll be OK. It'll just take time.'

Comfort nodded.

'Give our regards to your friends,' Daniel said.

He held out his hand and Comfort took it. He glanced at Corrina but neither of them made any motion towards the other. Daniel flicked the reins and the carriage drew away, raising dust. Comfort watched for a moment, then turned when he heard sounds in the doorway of the house. Annie was coming towards him, hobbling on her stick.

'Who is it?' she asked.

'Clayburne's folks.'

She looked after the retreating carriage.

'Why didn't you invite them in?' she said.

'They had other business. They couldn't stay,' he replied.

They stood together till the carriage disappeared from sight, then he put his arm around her shoulders.

'Come on,' he said. 'Let's go back and join the others.'